Tom Derringer
and the
Electrical Empire

Tom Derringer
and the
Electrical Empire

Lawrence Watt-Evans

Misenchanted Press

Bainbridge Island

This is a work of fiction. None of the characters and events portrayed in this novel are intended to represent actual person living or dead.

Tom Derringer and the Electrical Empire

Published by Misenchanted Press
www.misenchantedpress.com

Cover design by Lawrence Watt-Evans & Connie Hirsch
Frontispieces by Kyrith Evans

Dedicated to
Brenda & Larry Clough

"When I heaved my head and shoulders above that strip of tin and saw what lay beyond, though, it was nothing I had anticipated."

"...as we rounded a headland, I finally had a clear view. I stared, astonished, at the huge gray metal monstrosity chugging its way up the channel."

Chapter One

A Strange Encounter

As our train pulled into Philadelphia's Broad Street Station, Betsy Vanderhart and I sat silently in our compartment, somberly contemplating our situation.

We were returning from adventures out West, in California and the Utah Territory, but this was no joyous homecoming. We were rushing back to New Jersey because Betsy's father, the noted scientist Professor Aloysius Vanderhart of Rutgers College, had vanished, apparently kidnapped.

What's more, at least a dozen other scientists and adventurers had reportedly disappeared in the first three months of 1884. Adventurers, of course, disappeared quite often in pursuit of their adventures, sometimes returning unharmed after weeks or even years of silence, but there had been more of these disappearances than usual this year, and scientists did not ordinarily have any such propensity for vanishing without warning. We did not know for certain whether all these disappearances were related, but it did seem likely.

I knew little beyond these broad outlines. I did not even know the names of the men who had gone missing – or for that matter, whether they were all men; no one had mentioned that any women had disappeared, but no one had explicitly said otherwise, either. All we knew was from the brief reports from Mrs. Vanderhart's telegrams and casual mentions by my erstwhile employers.

The possibility that it might be best if I were to proceed directly to New York City had been considered. I might consult the Pierce Archives and talk to other professional adventurers there, to see whether anything more was known of the matter and get a grounding before tackling the specifics of Professor Vanderhart's case, but we had swiftly concluded that I should visit Betsy's home in New Brunswick first.

The first reason was that I would need to gather basic information about the professor's disappearance there sooner or later, and it might as well be sooner; that might not provide any insight into the other disappearances, but after all, I was only really looking for Professor Vanderhart, not for everyone who had gone missing. I would hear what the professor's family had to say, and would talk to the local police, and anyone else who might have witnessed anything relevant to the professor's abduction. It would be better, I thought, to start with the specifics and build out from there, rather than to start with generalities and try to narrow them down.

The second reason might seem of little import in comparison, but it was important to *me*. Betsy had asked me to accompany her to provide moral support for her meeting with her mother, as relations between the two had been severely strained of late. I could scarcely refuse; even though we had been in one another's company almost constantly for more than half a year, I still treasured every moment with her. Another man might exclaim upon her beauty – her golden locks, her petite figure, her heart-shaped face – but I most highly esteemed her good sense, her pluck, and her disdain for foolishness of any sort, most particularly my own. She had saved my life more than once and had protected me from my own inexperience and naivete.

I had once asked her to marry me, and she had told me not to be ridiculous. At the time I had not thought it ridiculous at all, and I still hoped that she might someday be my wife, but I knew that the circumstances of our acquaintance were such that she would not trust our feelings for one another until we had spent some time in ordinary civilized circumstances, rather than as prisoners of the lizard people in their tunnels beneath Los Angeles, or jammed into the smoky interior of a mechanical dinosaur in the Wasatch Mountains, or otherwise in mutual peril.

As a professional adventurer, though, I was not sure how much of my life would be spent in civilized circumstances.

I cannot say with any certainty what Betsy was thinking about as we arrived, but I supposed she was entirely concerned with her parents' situation. That I was more focused on my future with her than on how we might best find her father and restore him to the bosom of his family I found an embarrassing failure on my part. My best chance of winning her affections surely lay in finding her father, and perhaps the other missing scientists! But I had as yet little information upon which I might base my actions in that pursuit, and this lack of knowledge had allowed my mind to drift into other, more personal areas.

At any rate, we arrived in Philadelphia planning only a brief stop before boarding another train that would take us to New Brunswick. As the train came to a halt amid steam and smoke, I rose and offered Betsy my hand.

She ignored it, preferring to get to her feet unassisted, and led the way to the door. I followed her along the passage and out onto the platform, then paused to orient myself.

It was at that moment I heard someone call out, "Mr. Derringer!"

While I had made no particular effort to keep our movements secret, neither had I advertised them, and I was not expecting anyone to be looking for us at the station. For a moment I wondered whether the call was directed at someone else – after all, the famous gunsmith Henry Deringer had been based in Philadelphia; though he was long dead, some of his family surely remained. That seemed an unlikely coincidence, though. I turned to find the source of the voice, but my adventurer's training and recent experiences ensured that my right hand was under my coat, on the grip of my revolver, as I did. When I had headed West several months before I had kept my weapons packed away; I was no longer so confident I would not need them on short notice and carried my pistol at all times.

A stranger in an oddly cut jacket was waving at me from a dozen yards away. "Mr. Derringer!" he called again, as he started toward me. "Over here!"

He seemed to recognize my face, but I was fairly certain I had never seen him before. I was not completely unknown to some portions of the public, as my previous adventures had received some attention in the adventurers' community and the popular press, but I was not accustomed to being identified by strangers.

Betsy had heard the call, as well, of course, and had stepped aside, out of the stream of traffic, to a relatively quiet spot on the platform where she now appeared to be fumbling in her purse. I knew well that she did not actually *fumble* anywhere, and that this appearance was a deceit. I also knew she owned a small pistol, and that she knew how to use it.

The man who had called my name did not seem to have noticed Betsy at all, so I endeavored not to draw his attention to her; I looked directly at him and awaited his next action.

He beckoned to me, and after some hesitation, I warily approached him.

He was of moderate height, perhaps two or three inches shorter than myself, with broad shoulders and a neatly trimmed mustache. He wore one of those fashionable new Homburg hats on a head of sandy hair. He doffed this hat and said, "Thomas Derringer?"

"You have the advantage of me, sir," I said, as I stopped while still several feet away. I had to speak quite loudly to be heard over the noise of the station. My hand remained upon the grip of my pistol as I continued, "I don't believe we have met."

"We have not, sir, but it is an honor to finally have this opportunity." I could not place his accent, which was not

American, but he spoke well. "My name is Leopold de la Rue, and I have heard much about your recent adventures in Mexico. You have accomplished much for one so young!"

I had not been aware that my pursuit of Reverend Hezekiah McKee's aluminum airship was widely known. I frowned. "Should I recognize your name, Mr. de la Rue?"

He smiled wryly. "No, of course not, Mr. Derringer. I am merely a messenger, here on behalf of my employer, who provided me with a picture of you."

"And who might that employer be?"

"I am not at liberty to say, as yet. He has chosen to remain largely anonymous, operating out of the public view, but I believe you and he share certain interests."

"And what would those be?"

"I would prefer not to announce them to this entire crowd, Mr. Derringer. If you could perhaps accompany me to somewhere more private?"

I shook my head. "I am afraid I have other plans."

"My employer will happily pay you for your time."

That was moderately intriguing, but I had my promise to Betsy to fulfill. I shook my head again. "I cannot oblige you at this time, Mr. de la Rue; I have a prior obligation, and a train to catch. If you or your employer would like to send a letter to Mr. Tobias Arbuthnot in care of the Guaranty Trust Company, I will give it the closest attention when I have a few moments to spare."

"We would very much appreciate it if you could see your way clear to delay your other engagement, Mr. Derringer. I am authorized to offer you fifty dollars in gold for perhaps three hours of conversation, if you come immediately."

That was more than moderately intriguing; it was astonishing. In fact, it was so outrageous that it made me extremely suspicious. I could think of no reason anyone should pay such a preposterous sum simply for a few hours of my time.

Nonetheless, I could not take the time to investigate. "I am sorry I cannot oblige you," I replied. "I admit to considerable curiosity about your purpose, but regardless of anything you might offer, I must honor my existing commitment. Again, I suggest that a letter in Mr. Arbuthnot's care is your best approach, and for now I really must bid you farewell." I nodded, and turned away – but I kept my gun in my hand, in case Mr. de la Rue chose not to accept my refusal.

Betsy had faded into the milling crowds on the platform, and it took me a moment to locate her. When I did I made no effort to acknowledge her, but simply headed in the direction of our train to New Brunswick, trusting Betsy to join me along the way.

As, in fact, she did, and we boarded our coach without further incident and without conversation. Only when the conductor's whistle and shout of, "All aboard!" had sounded, and the huffing engine had set the train in motion, did we speak.

"What was *that* about?" Betsy asked, as I tucked my revolver securely away.

"He gave his name as de la Rue," I said, "and he offered me fifty dollars to accompany him for an interview with his employer, whose name he refused to divulge."

"*Fifty dollars*? It must be a trick."

"I thought that likely, yes."

"So that's why you turned him down? I'm surprised your curiosity did not prompt you to accept."

I shook my head. "I told you I would come with you to New Brunswick," I said.

"I..." She stopped, took a breath, and said, "So you did. But you are by nature impetuous, Tom, and I..." Once again, she left her sentence unfinished, and as the silence grew awkward, she turned to gaze out the window.

"I am a man of my word," I said, somewhat dismayed that she had thought I might break my promise.

"I know," she said, still looking away from me.

After that we did not speak for some time, but at last Betsy said, "How did he recognize you, did he say? Had you met before?"

I shook my head. "He said we had not, and I certainly don't remember him. He said his employer had provided a picture."

"His anonymous employer?"

I nodded.

"It seems very odd."

I could scarcely argue with that.

The train pulled into the station in New Brunswick perhaps twenty minutes behind schedule, and Betsy and I disembarked, our luggage delivered to the platform beside us. I engaged a porter to bring it out to the street, where I flagged down a hack.

Ten minutes later we climbed out in front of Professor Vanderhart's home. There Betsy hesitated, and I took it upon myself to step up to the front door and twist the bell handle.

A moment later the door opened, and there stood Mrs. Vanderhart. She stared at us silently for a moment, then burst into tears.

"Mother?" Betsy said, alarmed.

Her mother stepped aside, sobbing, and gestured for us to enter; we complied, first myself, and then Betsy. We took seats in the parlor and waited for our hostess to regain her composure.

It took several minutes, but at last she was able to say, "You're finally here!"

"Yes, Mother," Betsy said.

"You must find him!"

"We will do our best, Mrs. Vanderhart," I said, trying my best to sound reassuring. "Can you tell us what happened? Your telegrams did not give us very many details."

She took a deep breath to further control her emotions, and then began.

"Al got home safely from Sumatra in February, and..." She hesitated, glancing at her daughter. "Well, he was shocked that you weren't here. Your telegram in early March was a great relief to him, and we argued about whether we should reply, and what we should say, and... we didn't answer. I thought he might send you a wire himself, without telling me, but I guess he did not. I'm sorry. I still can't forgive...well, no. That's not true."

"Mrs. Vanderhart," I said gently. "Your husband?"

"Yes." She deliberately fixed her gaze on me, rather than Betsy. "All right. On the fifteenth of March we had a caller, a foreigner I think, someone the professor seemed to know, but I did not; if he gave his name I missed it, and Al didn't introduce us. You know how your father is, Elspeth. They spoke in his study for almost an hour, and when they emerged Al got his hat and coat and said he was going to walk our guest to the station. I told him dinner would be at seven, and he nodded, and they left, and I never saw him again."

I hesitated, then said, "Mrs. Vanderhart, in your telegram you did not say that your husband had *disappeared*; you said he had been *kidnapped*. Why did you use that word?"

"I was coming to that!" she exclaimed. "I was not worried when he didn't come home for dinner, because he had done that before when he lost track of time, but when he was not home by bedtime – well, he *hadn't* done *that* before. And when he still wasn't there in the morning, I went to the police and reported that he was missing. They started investigating, talking to people, and on Monday evening they told me that several witnesses had seen Al and his companion at the station, and that that man, whoever he was, had led Al to a buggy, where this man and the driver had grabbed Al and heaved him in and held him while the carriage drove off. He was *kidnapped*, Mr. Derringer! In fact, two of the witnesses went to the police themselves, but of course they didn't know who it was that had been taken, so it took a day or so before they realized it was the professor. And I talked to everyone, trying to make sense of it all, and I couldn't find out *anything*, so Tuesday afternoon I wired Betsy to come home and bring you with her, but then I didn't hear anything back for *two weeks*."

"We were up in the Wasatch Mountains, Mrs. Vanderhart;

I'm very sorry we missed your wire. Has there been any demand for a ransom?"

She shook her head vigorously. "*Nothing*, Mr. Derringer. There's been nothing."

"The police have made no progress?"

"None. I thought at first they were just keeping the investigation quiet, but Detective Morris told me that they were at a loss. No one recognized any of the men in the carriage, or at least no one will admit to it. I don't *understand*, Mr. Derringer; why would anyone take my Al?"

"I don't know, Mrs. Vanderhart." I hesitated. "Have you considered hiring a *private* investigator? Even if the police are stumped, I think someone trained in that field might do better than an adventurer such as myself."

"I don't *know* any investigators! I don't know whom I can trust! That man came to this house and behaved in a normal and respectable fashion, and then he lured the professor away and abducted him; how could I be sure that a stranger I hire isn't working for him?"

"Perhaps the Pinkertons..." I began.

"I think *not!*" she exclaimed. "Those blackguards would more likely get my Al killed than bring him home safely! No, he trusted *you*, Mr. Derringer, so I will do the same."

My own opinion of the Pinkerton organization was clearly more favorable than her own, even though I would concede they were hardly paragons of virtue. Still, I did not see any point in arguing. If I was unable to make any headway, I told myself, *I* could employ the Pinkertons or some other detective agency.

For the time being, though, I could at least take a look. "I'll do my best, Mrs. Vanderhart," I said.

Chapter Two

The Professor's Abduction

I did not really expect to learn anything at the railroad station; after all, weeks had passed, and the police had surely explored every inch of it long ago. Nonetheless on the Monday after our arrival, I looked it over carefully, accompanied by Detective Eli Morris of the New Brunswick city police. Mrs. Vanderhart had introduced us, and I found the detective a pleasant, if rather humorless, companion. Betsy accompanied us for two reasons; the stated one was that as she knew her father far better than either the detective or myself, she might spot traces we would miss. The more immediate reason was that I knew of no way short of physical violence to prevent her from doing so.

It was a dreary, overcast day, and Detective Morris said that on the afternoon of the fifteenth, the day that Professor Vanderhart had vanished, the weather had been similar – in fact, it had been raining intermittently.

The detective was kind enough to explain the entire series of events, as described by the various witnesses. Professor Vanderhart had been standing on the sidewalk under the station's overhang on Easton Street, staying out of the rain, and talking to a man none of the witnesses recognized, when a black buggy had pulled up beside them. The professor's companion had reached out and grasped the side of the buggy while the driver jumped down and joined him. The witnesses had described the driver as a virtual giant of a man, well over six feet in height and heavily muscled; he had advanced on the professor, but the professor had backed away, talking quietly – too quietly for anyone to make out what was said.

Then the two men had each grabbed one of Professor Vanderhart's arms and had pulled him into the buggy, an act that spoke well of their physical strength, given the professor's dimensions. They had heaved him aboard, then shoved him down on the seat between them, and while his erstwhile companion held him, the driver had whipped the horses, and the conveyance had rolled away with its three passengers. As he was hauled up into the buggy, Professor Vanderhart had cried out, and two witnesses claimed to have heard his exact words.

One had reported them to be, "What is this? This is a day you'll rue!"

The other had it as, "What is it? Mister, it's a day you'll rue!"

As soon as Detective Morris told us this, Betsy declared, "That can't be right."

Startled, the policeman looked at her. "Why not?" he said.

"My father wouldn't say that," she replied.

Detective Morris shook his head. "Miss, it's unusual that we have two listeners agree so closely on the exact words. I assure you, that is what they heard."

"Well, they heard wrong," she insisted. "I doubt my father has ever used the word 'rue' in his life."

"Perhaps it was a phrase he had recently picked up," I suggested.

"It wasn't."

"Betsy, we were gone for months, and your father had traveled halfway around the world to visit that volcanic island;

he might have changed."

"I don't believe it," she said. "They must have misheard him."

"Two respectable citizens agreed on the *very words*, Miss Vanderhart."

"But they didn't," I said. "Not exactly."

"They agreed on 'a day you'll rue,'" the detective said. "Neither budged from that under police questioning. We thought it a little melodramatic ourselves and suggested that perhaps he had said, 'You'll regret this,' or some such thing, but both of them, Mrs. Albright and Mr. Ferrillo, insisted on 'a day you'll rue.'"

"Well, leave it for now," I said, before Betsy could protest further. "What happened once he was in the buggy?"

"It rolled on around the corner onto Raritan Avenue, and away." He pointed, and led us in the direction indicated. "We tried to retrace its movements, Mr. Derringer, but one buggy looks much like another – our description had no distinctive details that might have allowed us to track it."

"And none of the witnesses thought to pursue it at the time?" Betsy asked.

"No, I am afraid they did not," Detective Morris replied. "You must recall, they were all at the station on their own business, it was raining, night was falling, and they had no idea who any of the individuals involved might be. More than one bystander assumed that your father was a criminal being apprehended by the police, though why anyone would think we would use a buggy rather than a proper police wagon I could not tell you."

"People often jump to conclusions without considering whether the details support them," I remarked. "It's something we adventurers struggle, not always successfully, to avoid."

I could see Betsy was suppressing an urge to reply to this. She was obviously not pleased with how her townsfolk had responded to her father's abduction, and I had the distinct impression she did not entirely believe the detective's version of events. She clearly found that phrase, "a day you'll rue," to be something less than credible, no matter how many witnesses might swear to it.

And, I suddenly realized, she might be right, though it would be a tremendous coincidence should my new supposition prove correct.

Or perhaps not a coincidence at all.

I had gotten a description of the professor's interlocutor from Mrs. Vanderhart, and another, substantially the same, from Detective Morris, and both could easily fit the man who had accosted me at Broad Street Station in Philadelphia. His size and coloring were not so distinctive that I had made the connection previously, but the professor's words fit so perfectly that I could not dismiss the similarity further.

"Detective," I said, "do you think those witnesses might have heard the professor exclaim, 'What is this, Mister de la Rue?'"

Startled, the detective stopped walking and turned to study my face. "What makes you suggest that, Mr. Derringer?"

"Because yesterday, in Philadelphia, I encountered a man calling himself Leopold de la Rue who offered me a large sum of money to agree to an interview with his employer. I understand that besides Professor Vanderhart, both scientists and adventurers have gone missing of late; perhaps, had I accepted his offer, I would have been one of them. The similarity of his name to the professor's reported words struck me."

"Leopold de la Rue," Detective Morris said thoughtfully.

"Do you know the name?" I asked.

He shook his head. "No, I'm afraid I do not. And officially, I can't confirm that any adventurers have gone missing. As I'm sure you understand, it's in the nature of the occupation for adventurers to come and go without warning, so we do not normally investigate such things. Scientists, though – if you'll agree to keep it under your hat, I'll tell you that the police have Thomas Edison under guard twenty-four hours a day."

I nodded. "Probably a wise precaution," I said. I glanced at Betsy, who was being uncharacteristically quiet, and found her staring intently at me. Slightly unnerved, I turned back to the detective.

"Then the New Brunswick police are aware of the disappearances and believe Professor Vanderhart's abduction to be connected?"

Mr. Morris hesitated. "'Believe' might be too strong," he said. "We are certainly aware of the possibility, though, and if your guess is right, and this de la Rue is involved - well, that would add a little more evidence to back up the notion. I'll want to put the word out that we'd like to talk to this fellow. What can you tell me about him?"

"Little you do not already know. Middling height, sandy hair, a little mustache. Solidly built but not especially stout - certainly not of Professor Vanderhart's girth. He had the manners of an educated man, not a hoodlum, and spoke with what I believe to be a European accent, though I could not place his nationality."

The detective pulled a pad from inside his jacket and noted my observations down. "That does accord with the descriptions we have received," he acknowledged.

As he wrote I looked around the street alongside the railway station. "I don't suppose there were any useful tracks, or other clues, to be found."

"Not a one," Detective Morris said, still writing. "We were fortunate to have so many witnesses! These fellows are audacious, certainly, to carry off Professor Vanderhart with half a dozen people watching. It's my understanding that nothing of the kind happened in any of the other disappearances, which is one reason we hesitate to say for certain that they're all the work of a single gang. Why this one should be different, if it's connected, we can't say. And for one of the kidnappers to use the same name here and in Philadelphia, if that *is* what happened, is remarkably careless for a group that has otherwise left no trace." He finished his note and tucked pen and pad away.

"A good point," I acknowledged. Again, I looked at Betsy, who was now staring into the distance and biting her lower lip.

That was not at all her usual behavior. I concluded that she had, for some reason, resolved to say nothing more in the detective's presence.

We had reached the corner of the station, and I looked down the street where the buggy had last been seen. I saw nothing distinctive or useful; it led down a gentle slope to a bridge across the Raritan River.

"I suppose they could have been headed anywhere on the far side of the river," I said.

"Indeed. As far as their destination is concerned, your guess is as good as mine," Detective Morris replied.

I did not think that was literally true, since I knew very little of the city's geography, but I did not argue. "I assume that if they were bound for New York City, this would have been their best route."

"Yes, but they would need to get the ferry from Jersey City. That's better than thirty miles, which would be a great deal to ask of their horse. They could not have reached Manhattan until well into the following day – Sunday the 16th, or even Monday."

"Oh, of course." I started to say something about boarding a train further up the line, but then decided against it. Surely, a professional detective would have already considered these possibilities!

"Have you made any inquiries along the way?" I asked instead.

"We have sent notices to every police agency from here to Connecticut," he replied. "As yet, we have not a single useful response."

I nodded, then risked another glance at my companion. Betsy's face was quite expressionless.

"Is there anything else you think we should know, Detective?"

"Can't think of anything, Mr. Derringer."

"Betsy, do you have any questions you'd like to ask?"

She glared at me. "No," she said.

I had no idea what had so upset her, and decided that finding out was more important than further conversation with Detective Morris. "Thank you, Detective," I said, taking his hand. We shook. "I won't keep you any longer; I appreciate your generosity in giving us so much of your time."

"Oh, it's nothing, Mr. Derringer. After all, we want to know what's become of Professor Vanderhart almost as much as you do! I'll let you know if we know anything about this...Leonard? No, Leopold de la Rue. That's right, is it?"

"Exactly right, Detective. Thank you again." I withdrew my hand, and then turned away, letting Betsy take my arm as we headed back toward her family home.

Once I was quite sure we were out of earshot of the detective, I asked, "Betsy, what's the matter? Why didn't you want to talk to Detective Morris?"

"I don't trust him, Tom," she said. "There's something about all this that makes me suspicious. Half a dozen people saw my father kidnapped, but did nothing to stop it? No one ever suspected something was wrong with that 'day you'll rue' nonsense? Honestly, Tom, who speaks like that outside cheap melodramas?"

"I think some people really do, but I take your point – I would expect someone being kidnapped to say something more along the lines of, 'What are you doing?' But Detective Morris..."

"Tom, stop. It's plain to me that there is some sort of organization at work here. De la Rue and an accomplice kidnapped my father – assuming, of course, we can believe *anything* the detective told us. Mr. de la Rue tried to intercept you at the station in Philadelphia. There are the other missing scientists and adventurers. This isn't a coincidence, Tom; this is a *conspiracy*, and we don't know who might be involved in it. Might it be that the reason the police have made no progress is that they are being betrayed by their own men? Could *Detective Morris* be working for the same people who ordered my father's abduction? It was when I saw that possibility, and could not dismiss it or even think it particularly unlikely, that I stopped taking part in the discussion. When you volunteered Mr. de la Rue's name – well, I wish you had not. I had already resolved to say as little as possible to avoid giving away anything that might aid our foes, and there you were, happily revealing something that might be important. Tom, we can't trust *anyone* until we know what's happening!"

I took a deep breath and gathered my thoughts before I replied.

"Betsy," I said, "you have often told me that I am too trusting, and I must acknowledge that this has sometimes been a very real failing on my part. I *have* been too trusting, though I like to think I'm improving. However, in *this* case, I think you have gone too far in the opposite direction. Yes, I believe there is a conspiracy afoot, and we do not know its extent or its purpose. There may indeed be conspirators within the police department. But we cannot treat *everyone* with nothing but suspicion; we will be unable to accomplish anything if we do not dare speak with the people we meet in the course of our investigation. Should we encounter a member of the conspiracy, we may well learn as much from his questions and falsehoods as he does from our replies."

"That may be true, Tom; I can see your reasoning. But I was not prepared to go on chatting with that detective when I realized he might well be working with the conspirators." She shuddered, then said, "Perhaps next time, now that I know we must be vigilant, I will be able to behave in a more normal manner."

I nodded at that. Then I continued casually, "If Detective Morris is indeed a part of the conspiracy, do you think he would have quoted those two witnesses? Surely he would have known that I was to have met Mr. de la Rue in Philadelphia; would he not worry that I might make precisely the connection that I did in fact make?"

Betsy started to answer, then stopped and considered for a few seconds.

"I don't know," she said at last. "If we are truly determined not to trust anyone, how do we even know there *were* any witnesses, let alone that they reported what Detective Morris said they did?"

"But then why would he tell us such a tale?"

"To make you seek out de la Rue, perhaps. It might be a trap."

"The possibility that de la Rue meant to lure me into a trap had already occurred to me."

She was silent for a few seconds, then said, "Will you look for him anyway?"

"We have no other leads at all, so far as I can see, so unless you have a better idea, yes, I will."

We walked on for another block and were almost on her family's doorstep when she said, "I won't come with you this time."

"I think that's wise," I said. "I'm sure you are weary of adventuring."

"More than that, my mother needs me," she replied. "And I cannot trust my own reactions when this matter strikes so close to home – you are quite right, I *did* overreact to my doubts about Detective Morris."

I nodded. "But I hope, dear Betsy, that you will serve as my reserve force, should I need one. If I am indeed taken and do not return after a certain time, perhaps a fortnight, I want you to make contact with my mother, and Tobias Arbuthnot, and Mad Bill Snedeker, and anyone else you can think of who might come to my aid. I am not eager to be held captive again, and I have noticed in my study of my father's journals and other tales of adventurers that those who operate in a group, as my father did in Darien Lord's band, tend to fare better than those who insist on working alone. I do not yet have an entire band of adventurers supporting me, but I do have *you*, and you are worth as much as to me as a dozen men."

"That's nonsense," she said. "But I will do what I can."

Chapter Three

Strands of the Web

The man who called himself Leopold de la Rue had not given me his card, or any way to reach him – a fact that began, in the atmosphere of heightened wariness that surrounded our situation, to appear suspicious, though it might well simply have been caused by the hurried circumstances of our encounter. I had, however, given *him* a way to find *me*, through Tobias Arbuthnot. I determined to pay my family's banker a visit at the first opportunity and alert Mr. Arbuthnot to the situation. I had been staying at a small hotel near the Rutgers campus, but after my meeting with Detective Morris I told Mrs. Vanderhart that I did not think I could learn any more in New Brunswick, though I thought I had a possible lead elsewhere. I did not say any more than that; I told her I could not be sure whether there might be unwelcome listeners, and she immediately agreed to press me no further.

Mother and daughter were both now living in a state of extreme suspicion. Until now I had never seen much resemblance between Betsy and her mother, but this terrible set of circumstances had induced a remarkable similarity of thought. Both were now so concerned with the professor's fate that their own previous dispute had faded away to almost nothing.

Accordingly, I had few reservations about leaving Betsy in

her family home while I resumed my journey to New York. I was able to make a few purchases before catching my train, at last replacing the hat I had lost in the Utah Territory, so I felt rather more myself when I reached the city. I arrived at my usual accommodation, the Robertson Hotel, without incident, and then, although the afternoon was well advanced, I took a hansom cab to Mr. Arbuthnot's establishment, hoping to catch him before he left for the day.

As it happens, I arrived at his Madison Avenue office just as he was packing up for the day, about to head out for his supper. His secretary, after a moment's hesitation and a display of reluctance, allowed me in. I suppose the reluctance was because my presence meant he could not yet leave for his own evening meal.

Tobias Arbuthnot looked up at the opening door and stopped dead when he saw me.

He looked very much as I remembered him, though he had trimmed his narrow beard down to a stub; he was a small man, severely dressed, with his black hair slicked back and his cheeks clean shaven, but I knew his appearance was at odds with his warm personality. After a second's pause, he exclaimed, "Tom!" as he resumed his motion and stepped toward me, a broad smile upon his narrow face. I think only the briefcase in his hand prevented him from flinging his arms around me in a cordial embrace, or making some other extravagant gesture. "*This* is a fortunate encounter! I have just this afternoon received a letter for you."

"Indeed," I replied. "From a Mr. de la Rue, perhaps?"

"Ah, you were expecting it?" The smile dimmed a trifle.

"Say, rather, I cannot think offhand of anyone else who might write to me in your care, where I suggested exactly that to this de la Rue just three days ago."

"Oh, I see. Well, I have it right here, so let me deliver it to you now." He plucked an envelope from the rack on his desk and proffered it. I accepted it, and glanced at the address – Thomas Derringer, care of Tobias Arbuthnot, Guaranty Trust Company, from Leopold de le Rue, General Delivery, Cape May, New Jersey.

Cape May? I had rather assumed that if he gave any return address at all, it would be in Philadelphia. I filed that away mentally while I tucked the letter itself into an inside pocket.

"Thank you," I said. "I do hope you don't mind my imposing on you in this fashion."

"Mind? Good heavens, no! Not at all. Surely you know that I hold you and your mother and sister in the highest esteem and am happy to assist you in whatever way I can."

"I had thought you disapproved of my chosen career."

"Oh, I do! I think it a grave mistake to put yourself at risk in a career of adventure when you have no need to do so. But that hardly means that I do not wish you every felicity and all good fortune; indeed, you need it all the more! Given the nature of your employment, to refuse you my aid in even the most trivial matter might prove to have grave consequences indeed." He hesitated, and then asked, "Is this letter perhaps connected with some new adventurous undertaking?"

"It may be," I admitted. "I am not yet entirely certain of its relevance."

"Is it what brought you to me, or was there some other business you wished to transact?"

"I had indeed come to inquire after the letter; I would not have brought any more complex matter here at so late an hour. Well, that, and to let you know that I am in town once more. But pray, do not let me detain you; I'm sure you want your supper."

"Oh, I can always spare a little time for you, my boy."

I glanced over my shoulder. "I am not sure your secretary feels the same."

His gaze followed my own. "Ah," he said. Then he called, "Mr. Harris, there is no need for you to stay; I will lock up."

"As you please, sir," the secretary replied.

"Now, Tom...but wait. Have you any dinner plans?"

I admitted I did not.

"Then perhaps you might join me at my club – we have recently relocated, and I would be delighted to show you our splendid new home. You can tell me about your adventures out West, and if it is not too delicate a matter perhaps you can explain this letter. In return, I would be happy to review for you the status of your family's investments, though of course I will not have every detail on hand."

"I would be delighted, Mr. Arbuthnot," I replied.

"Toby, please." He transferred his briefcase to his other hand and retrieved a set of keys from his pocket, and we left his office, locking it securely behind us.

I had not, until this occasion, ever eaten at a gentlemen's club. Mr. Arbuthnot's was the University Club, on the avenue just a few blocks to the south, and its building was, as he had said, quite a splendid establishment, only recently acquired. I enjoyed the experience very much, despite the unfortunate circumstances that had brought me there. Over a fine leg of lamb I told him about my journey to California, carefully omitting a good many names and other details, and about the errand I ran in the Utah Territory, again leaving out those portions I thought it unwise to reveal. He fully understood my reasons for circumspection and did not press me to fill in any gaps.

For his part, as dish followed dish he gave me a quick summary of my family's holdings, and some information on the current sad state of the national economy. Due to the conservative nature of my family's investments, we stood in a better position than most, but my profligate spending on my adventures had significantly stressed our finances. For the most part I had blithely ignored this, too involved with my own concerns to really even notice the economic depression that had begun about the same time I set out to find the mystery airship seen in the Arizona skies. I resolved to take these matters more seriously in the future.

He plunged on into details of Wall Street's current slump, an unrelenting stream of names and numbers that left my head spinning without really giving me any greater comprehension of the situation than I had had when we first sat down, save perhaps that if I understood correctly, too many people had continued to invest in railroad construction despite a dearth of profitable routes that were not already adequately serviced. Several banks and brokerages were said to be in danger of collapse; there were rumors that even the firm of Grant & Ward, in which General Grant himself and his eldest son were partners, was insolvent, or close to it. Mr. Arbuthnot had thought it prudent to withdraw all his clients' investments, including my family's, from any institutions he considered to be even remotely at risk.

He also explained, in passing, why he had cut his beard back from its former length to its present reduced state – he had managed to set it aflame at a moment when such a distraction was most extraordinarily unwelcome. His recounting of this incident, where every mishap had been followed by even greater disaster, set me laughing so vigorously I could not hold my dessert fork and needed a few minutes to regain my composure.

And finally, as he settled back with his cigar – I had politely declined the one he had offered me, as I had never cultivated an interest in tobacco – we came to the question of Mr. de la Rue's letter. I described my encounter on the platform in Philadelphia and explained what Detective Morris had told us of Professor Vanderhart's abduction.

"So, this letter is from your mysterious stranger?"

"And quite possibly Professor Vanderhart's abductor, yes."

"What else do you know of him?"

"Nothing, as yet."

"You haven't consulted Dr. Pierce? Or Mr. Snedeker?"

"Not yet; I had intended to start with a visit the Pierce Archives tomorrow. I had not thought to visit Mad Bill any time soon."

"Well, the Archives are certainly more likely to be of help, but I would talk to Mr. Snedeker as well; he has been involved with adventurers for more than three decades now, and has a prodigious memory for the names and details he comes across."

"*Does* he?" I asked, startled.

"Oh, yes. You might think him little more than a buffoon, but that is an appearance he has deliberately assumed, to encourage others to underestimate him. As I once heard the man himself phrase it, he may be mad, but he's no fool."

"I knew he was no fool," I said. "I have read my father's journals, after all, and I know that both my father and Mr. Lord held him in high esteem, but I had thought that was more for his quick wits and physical gifts than for any remarkable memory."

"He does not advertise it, but I have known him for almost twenty years, and I have seen it."

"Thank you for the suggestion, then; I will look into it. But I will begin with the Pierce Archives."

"Of course, of course!" He took a puff on his cigar, and I thought that perhaps it was time for me to take my leave. I pushed back my chair.

"Oh, but Tom!" he exclaimed, almost dropping his cigar. "Surely you aren't going to leave before you read your letter?"

"What?"

"I realize it may contain information you don't care to share, but won't you at least open it and see what it says before we part?"

"I did not want to appear rude by reading it in front of you." In truth, I had been so caught up in our conversation that I had almost forgotten its presence.

"Nonsense! Please do read it; for all we know it may have

some urgent information to impart regarding Professor Vanderhart's present circumstances."

"I suppose it might, at that." I reached into my pocket and drew out the envelope, then slit it open with my pen knife.

The letter within was a single page, written in a clear but inelegant hand.

"Dear Mr. Derringer," I read. "My employer has authorized me to explain in somewhat more detail what he hopes to learn from you. While we are not in a position to impose any requirements upon you, we hope you will keep this in the strictest confidence. He would like to learn everything you can tell him of the Reverend Hezekiah McKee's experiences in the Lost City of the Mirage, and any information you may have on what he brought away from that City. He has no interest in intruding upon your privacy in other matters. You are free to refuse, of course, and need not respond to questions you would prefer not to answer. If you will agree to an interview, at a time and place of your choosing, the offer of fifty dollars in gold as compensation for your time still stands. You may write to me at the address above, or for a more immediate response you may leave a message at the Hotel Brunswick at 225 Fifth Avenue."

It was signed, with a rather clumsy flourish, "Leopold de la Rue."

I did not quote any of this to my host. Instead, when I had finished reading I looked up from the letter and said, "It would seem that our conspirators are in pursuit of a particular familiar mystery, though they ask me not to reveal which one."

"And does this explain their interest in Professor Vanderhart?"

"It does not. In fact, I begin to doubt whether there is indeed a connection. Perhaps our Mr. de la Rue is a freelance operative who has been hired for two unrelated tasks that are only linked by my coincidental involvement."

"Then the professor has no connection with this mystery

you do not name?"

"None that I know of." A thought struck me. "But he recently took an extended trip to the South Seas; perhaps he encountered something there that interested Mr. de la Rue. Do you know whether anything remarkable has been reported in the Dutch East Indies in the last several months? Besides last year's volcanic eruption, that is."

"I have no idea. I'm afraid I do not keep up with the news of the adventurers' fraternity, even though I have half a dozen among my clients."

"Hmm." This was something else I would want to ask Dr. Pierce – *had* the Lost City been seen in the area the professor visited? I had not heard of its manifestation anywhere since its 1880 appearance in the Arizona Territory. I recalled that there had been predictions its next visit might be in the South Pacific, but I was fairly sure that was not expected to occur for some months yet.

Perhaps there *was* a connection between Betsy's father and the Lost City. I wondered whether Mrs. Vanderhart would know. I now had even more questions for Dr. Pierce.

"Am I to understand that Mr. de la Rue's anonymous employer seeks an interview?" Mr. Arbuthnot asked.

"Indeed, he does."

"And will you oblige him in this fashion?"

"It is an interesting thing, Toby, that submitting to questioning can often be a highly educational experience. One learns a great deal from what questions are asked, and how they are phrased. The interviewer's interests and assumptions are often surprisingly plain."

"Then you will."

"I think so, yes."

"Be careful, Tom. If these people kidnapped Professor Vanderhart, they are dangerous and not to be trusted."

"Don't worry, sir. I know that, and will take every

precaution." With that, I pushed back my chair and rose. "It has been a genuine pleasure to speak with you at such length, Toby – not to mention this magnificent repast you have furnished, or the generosity you have displayed in bringing me to this fine establishment." I held out my hand. "Thank you, and I hope the next such occasion will not be long in coming."

He rose as well, and we shook.

He turned me over to an attendant who showed me to the door, and I emerged onto Madison Avenue to find the evening well advanced, and the air surprisingly chilly for the second half of April. I turned up my collar and set out for the Robertson Hotel.

As I walked, I considered what I had learned, and what I should do about it.

Clearly, I would begin by consulting Dr. Pierce. I would be giving him the details of my adventures in California and the Utah Territory, and in return he would answer my questions. I had thought those questions would be about the missing scientists and adventurers, about Leopold de la Rue, and about Professor Vanderhart, but now I knew I also wanted to learn as much as possible about the Lost City of the Mirage, and about those who were obsessed with it. I knew a few names – Giuseppe Spinelli and Dieter Hammerschlag had studied its movements in some depth and devised theories intended to predict when and where it would reappear, but I knew almost nothing else about them. I had heard that many believed the Barnstable-Gomez model was just as sound as either Spinelli's or Hammerschlag's, but I had no idea who Barnstable and Gomez might have been, or whether they still lived.

In my first visit to the Archives two years before, I had spoken at length with a man named Gerhardt von Düssel who had visited the Lost City in its 1880 appearance. And of course, the late Reverend Hezekiah McKee had obtained the aluminum for his airship there.

Might Hammerschlag, or Spinelli, or von Düssel be among the missing scientists and adventurers?

Before I read Mr. de la Rue's letter I had no idea what steps I might take to locate Professor Vanderhart, but now at least I had more questions to ask.

I walked through the lobby of the Robertson Hotel completely lost in my own thoughts and went directly to my room and to bed.

Chapter Four

At the Archives

I awoke bright and early the next morning, undertook my morning ablutions, then donned the best clothes I had with me, and went down to breakfast at the hotel's restaurant. My original intention had been to be waiting at the door of the Pierce Archives when they opened for the day, but as I ate I reconsidered and resolved to do a little shopping first. I set out for R.H. Macy's renowned Sixth Avenue establishment.

It was therefore around ten o'clock when I finally stepped into the Archives carrying a thick notebook, wearing my new derby, and with a fine, freshly purchased fountain pen in my pocket. I looked up and down the length of the extraordinarily long counter that separated the customers from the Archives proper; there were fewer than a dozen people bent over various tomes and documents. I was mildly surprised to see that one was a woman; while I certainly knew that female adventurers existed, since my own mother had been one in her youth, I had not been aware that any had accounts with Dr. Pierce.

I found a place at an unused blotter not far from the window at the west end, where I perched on the stool, opened my notebook and took out my new pen, and then waited for one of the attendants to notice me.

A young man of about my own age came up and whispered cheerfully, "Good morning, sir! Do you have a membership?"

"I do," I said. "My name is John Thomas Derringer. If he's

not too busy, I would greatly appreciate speaking to Dr. Pierce himself."

"I will see if he's available, Mr. Derringer."

"Thank you."

The fellow bustled away, and I had scarcely had a chance to glance out at Lafayette Street when Dr. Pierce appeared from somewhere in the maze of shelves and presented himself.

"Mr. Derringer," he said. "How may I be of service?"

"I have several questions, Dr. Pierce. Rather than ask you to stand there bending over the counter for all of them, perhaps there is somewhere we can both sit?"

"Do not trouble yourself, sir." He reached back and pulled a stool from somewhere – I did not see exactly where – and seated himself opposite me. "Now, what did you want to know?"

"Well, as you may be aware, I am newly returned from a trip to the West, and I assume you would be interested in adding an account of my experiences to your Archives."

"Indeed, if your activities are of concern to adventurers, I would be very interested. Did you keep a journal, as your father did?"

I shook my head. "No, I am afraid I did not. I attempted to, but I discovered it to be very difficult to record one's adventures while they are still happening, and even more difficult to keep such a record secure; after losing one journal in Mexico and one in California, and being unable to replace them promptly, I concluded that it was not practical to keep a contemporary account. I have no idea how my father managed it. I have trained myself in remembering details, though, and I believe I can produce an accurate description of my journeys. I wrote notes for myself on the train East, as well, though those are not in a state I am willing to share, and I will use those in preparing my reports. However, there is a complication – I have promised certain parties that I would not reveal certain information about them. Will this be a problem?"

Dr. Pierce pursed his lips. "As I am sure you understand, I would prefer an unexpurgated account."

"Of course. But would an abridged version still be of interest?"

"What is it you propose to omit?"

"The exact location of particular installations and possibly the identities of certain participants."

He sighed. "I will take whatever you are willing to provide and credit it to your account."

I nodded. "That will be entirely satisfactory. Now, if I might draw on that credit – well, let me start by simply satisfying my own curiosity on a few points. This may actually have some effect on what I can tell you, now that I think about it."

"And what would these points be?"

"Are you aware of a committee based in San Francisco that monitors the activities of adventurers in their area?" I had never heard of the nameless committee until my adventures in California, but they had hired me some six weeks earlier to locate a missing man. I thought that Dr. Pierce might be interested in them, if he was not already familiar with their operations, but I was unsure how much I should reveal.

"Oh, of course! Messrs. Murray, Holzmann, Dobbs, Cartwright, Clement, and Stanford. They have sometimes hired my customers, and we have on occasion shared informants."

I had not been aware that anyone named Stanford was involved and wondered whether this would be the famous Mr. Leland Stanford, but I decided not to mention that. Mr. Murray had told me that there were only five permanent members, but perhaps he had preferred not to involve this Mr. Stanford, or perhaps Dr. Pierce's sources were in error. "Ah," I said. "Then I need not be over cautious in discussing the business I had with them."

"I should think not. What else?"

"Have you heard from Teddy Hancock recently?" Teddy

Hancock was the adventurer the committee had hired me to find after he went missing in the Utah Territory.

"Not directly. I am aware he has returned safely from his venture into the Wasatch Mountains."

"You knew he was there?"

"Of course."

"Do you know what he was doing there?" He had been investigating reports of living dinosaurs, but the committee had not wanted that known.

"I have been asked not to share that information."

"As have I."

"It would be interesting to know whether our stories match."

"I would guess they do," I said, but as it was only a guess, I determined to reveal as little as possible of Teddy's mission. "But I think that's enough about my western adventures for now; let us turn to other, more pressing matters. I assume you are aware that several scientists and adventurers have gone missing in recent months?"

"Indeed. I understand one of them, Professor Aloysius Vanderhart, to be an acquaintance of yours. Is it his abduction that brings you here?"

"It is," I said.

"I will provide what information I can, Mr. Derringer, but let me tell you now that I do not know what has become of him, nor of any of the others, and neither do I know with any degree of certainty what the connections among the missing might be."

"But you know who they are? The missing scientists, I mean?"

"I have a list of eleven scientists, though I believe it to be far from complete. I am unable to give as precise a count of missing adventurers, for obvious reasons, but there are at least three whose departures were under suspicious circumstances."

"Does your list include Giuseppe Spinelli or Dieter Hammerschlag?"

"I see you may know more about this than I had expected. Dr. Spinelli has indeed vanished. But at last report, Professor Hammerschlag was still safe in Munich."

"Are any of the others known to have some association with the Lost City of the Mirage?"

"I would say that Mr. Aubrey Elliot fits that description, yes. He visited the City in North Africa in 1873, in pursuit of evidence for his theories on electrical fields. And one of the missing adventurers is Peter Kirk, the only man to visit the City twice. At the age of eighty-one he is long since retired from adventuring, of course, which is why his disappearance is considered highly suspicious."

I quickly recorded those names in my notebook. "And the rest of the scientists?" I asked.

"Most of them are known for their work with electricity; Dr. Spinelli and Professor Vanderhart are the exceptions. None of them are known to have visited the City, and I am not aware of any less direct connections." He frowned. "To be honest, Mr. Derringer, I am not sure whether Professor Vanderhart's abduction is part of the same phenomenon that has resulted in the other disappearances. He had not made any discoveries concerning electricity; his areas of interest primarily had to do with gases under pressure and simple mechanics. He had no association with the Lost City that I am aware of. All the others had some connection with either electricity or the City. He is very much the odd man out and the reason I say I do not know what connections there might be among the missing."

That was interesting. He was also the only one who was known, beyond question, to have been forcibly abducted. Perhaps his kidnapping was mere coincidence and not part of some great conspiracy - but if so, that made it all the more baffling! Why would anyone want poor Professor Vanderhart?

And de la Rue's letter made it clear that his employer was very interested in the Lost City, even if that did not explain why he would want the professor. Perhaps there was some connection after all, just not one as obvious as the others.

"Then there is no news of the Lost City appearing in the South Seas while Professor Vanderhart was visiting that region? I understood one prediction had said it might manifest there."

"The Barnstable–Gomez hypothesis does predict that, but even should their calculations prove correct it is not due for several months yet, and I have not heard any news to suggest it has appeared there."

Well, that was fairly conclusive; such news certainly *would* reach Dr. Pierce if it were generally known. "What of Gerhardt von Düssel?" I asked. "Is he among the missing adventurers?"

"I have not heard from him recently, but I am not aware that he has been reported missing."

I decided it was time to move on, and to approach the issue from another angle. "Have you ever heard of a man named Leopold de la Rue?" I asked.

"Of course," Dr. Pierce replied. "He is a regular customer of mine. Would you like to arrange a meeting?"

I blinked. I realized, though, that I should not have been surprised; if de la Rue's employer was interested in the Lost City of the Mirage, of course he would have consulted the Pierce Archives, either directly or through a proxy. It was perhaps the greatest depository of information on the subject in the world.

"I have met him," I said, "just a few days ago. Indeed, I have a letter from him in my pocket. I know almost nothing about him, though."

Dr. Pierce nodded. "He may well be in this afternoon, should you care to speak with him."

"I think not just yet," I said. "What can you tell me about him, without breaching any confidences? Is he an adventurer?"

"I do not believe he is, though he certainly takes an interest in the adventurer's trade. He seems to be acting as a professional researcher for his employer – a Frenchman by the name of

Sebastien Boireau. Monsieur Boireau purchased a membership in, oh, 1871, I think it was, just after the great Franco–Prussian War. He used it sporadically himself for some time – I had the impression he was not in New York very often – but about six years ago he asked me to transfer it to Mr. de la Rue, who has been coming in frequently ever since."

"May I ask how he paid for his membership?"

"By monthly bank drafts, drawn on the Marine National Bank of New York."

That was rather more specific than I had expected or desired. "I meant, did he offer any information in exchange for your services?"

"No, he did not. As I said, I do not believe Mr. de la Rue to be an adventurer, and the same applies to Monsieur Boireau. I think you may not realize, Mr. Derringer, how unusual you are in receiving a membership by barter, rather than by paying cash."

In fact, I had not realized it was at all out of the ordinary; I had assumed it to be the norm. When I took a moment to think about it, though, I realized that Dr. Pierce could hardly have afforded to maintain and operate his archives without customers who paid in dollars, rather than stories of adventure. "I see," I said. I hesitated. "I hope I am not overstepping the bounds of propriety, but can you tell me whether Mr. de la Rue's interests are primarily concerned with the history of the Lost City?"

"As he has made no attempt to disguise his interests, nor requested confidentiality, I think I am free to say that the Lost City is almost the *only* subject of his inquiries, and of Monsieur Boireau's before him. Why do you ask? Do you think that Mr. de la Rue may be at risk of disappearing?"

"On the contrary, I fear he may be among those *responsible* for the disappearances."

"Oh, dear." He sighed. "How sound is your basis for this suspicion?"

I hesitated. I remembered Betsy's insistence that we could

not trust *anyone*, but surely that did not extend to Dr. John Pierce. Still, I did not want to spread any rumors.

And I did wonder why, if my suspicions were correct, no one else appeared to be investigating Mr. de la Rue in connection with the missing scientists. Was it because I had stumbled across the link to Professor Vanderhart's abduction when no one else had? Or was there some exculpatory evidence I had missed?

"That's hard to say," I answered. "It's entirely possible someone is deliberately misleading me, or that the apparent connection is merely a bizarre coincidence." It would be a most remarkable coincidence indeed, given the match of appearance and the recurring name.

"I would be interested in anything more you can tell me, of course."

"Of course, but at present I am not ready to say any more."

"In the interest of the safety of my clients, I hope you will forgive me if I mention your suspicion should the subject arise. I will not cite you as my source, naturally."

I frowned. I did not want to spread any baseless rumors, but my concerns about Mr. de la Rue were *not* baseless, and such a warning might prevent an abduction. "I will trust your discretion," I said.

"Thank you. Was there anything else?"

I gave the matter some thought and asked a few further questions of little consequence. I ascertained that the Leopold de le Rue who was a regular customer of the Archives matched precisely the description of the man who had approached me in Philadelphia, right down to having recently acquired a Homburg hat of which he was quite fond, as well as the description of the professor's abductor. I also learned that there was no recent news of the Lost City – none, really, since its appearance outside Flagstaff in 1880. Nothing new had been learned about its nature, its origins, or when and where it might next manifest itself.

Shortly before noon I could think of nothing more to ask; I closed my notebook and rose.

As I was leaving the building after I had bid Dr. Pierce farewell it occurred to me that perhaps I should have asked whether anything unusual was known to be happening in the vicinity of Cape May, since de la Rue had given that as his address, but I decided that it was not worth going back upstairs to make such an inquiry.

Chapter Five

My Interview with Monsieur Boireau

I surprised Mad Bill Snedeker with a lunchtime visit to his Perry Street saloon, Snedeker's Tavern & Billiard Emporium, where he greeted me with astonishing enthusiasm. It seemed he had not heard of my return to eastern climes, so my sudden unheralded appearance was completely unexpected. His employee, Mr. Dobbs, was left to deal with the lunchtime crowd – if eight or nine scruffy workmen can be said to constitute a crowd – while Mr. Snedeker and I retreated to the room behind the tavern.

I wondered idly whether this Mr. Dobbs was related in any way to Mr. Dobbs of Sacramento, who was one member of the committee that had hired me to find a lost adventurer in the Utah Territory. Dr. Pierce's list of the committee's members had reminded me of the similarity of names. I suspected that this New York Dobbs was not related to the man in California, or at least not closely enough to matter, but it was a mildly interesting coincidence, all the same.

When we had settled down at the table and the harried Mr. Dobbs had provided us with beer and sandwiches, Mad Bill opened the conversation with a direct question: "So, boy, have you come to your senses and had enough of adventuring, then?"

I smiled ruefully. "No, Uncle Bill, I'm afraid not. In fact, I've come to you in part to see if you have any information that might be of use in my current adventure."

"You're on one right now? Damn it, Tom! Haven't you just got back from one, and you've already started another?"

"I'm afraid so. A friend's father has been abducted, and I have promised to do what I can to bring him home safely."

"Abducted? Then at least you have a bloody good *reason* this time! Tell me what's happened."

I recounted the story Detective Morris had told us and explained my deduction that Leopold de la Rue was responsible for Professor Vanderhart's kidnapping.

"Would you, perhaps, know Mr. de la Rue? Dr. Pierce tells me he has been a regular at the Archives for some years now."

"De la Rue?" Mad Bill said, stroking his generous beard thoughtfully. "I don't think I do. The name doesn't ring any bells. Of course, I might have met him under another name."

I had not considered that. I frowned, and asked, "What about his employer, a Frenchman by the name of Sebastien Boireau?"

"Sebastien Boireau? Sure, I know him! Or at least, I know who he is; I haven't met him. He's been hiring adventurers for the last few years, for this and that, so his name's come up in here a few times."

This news was a pleasant surprise. "*Has* it? Who has he hired, and for what?"

"Well, he paid Little Alvin - that's Alvin Hennessy, from Virginia - to fetch him back some mystical thingamajig from Tibet, but I don't think Alvin ever found it. In fact, last I heard, Alvin hadn't ever come back, and his partner Big Roscoe Doolittle was pretty upset about it."

"Who else?"

"Let's see - he sent Janie Pederson to talk some Russian scientist into...well, something, anyway, Janie wouldn't give any details. She got whatever it was she was after, but she didn't like the way Boireau treated her. And there were the Bianchi brothers; they just disappeared last year, and Enzio's wife came in here wanting to know whether I'd heard anything from them and whether I knew anything about this Boireau."

That was a rather high percentage of former employees who had not come back, even for adventurers, and Miss Pederson's reported attitude was not encouraging. "He does not sound like a pleasant fellow," I ventured.

"I'd say that's putting it mildly. My understanding is that he's one of these grand gentlemen so set on helping mankind that he doesn't have any time for people."

"But *does* he mean to help mankind?"

"So he says – or so I'm told; as I said, I've never met him."

"He's not simply trying to make a fortune for himself?"

"Oh, he *has* a damn fortune! I don't know the details, but he seems to be rolling in it. Family money, I think. That's one reason people who ought to know better keep working for him – he pays well. And he actually pays what he says he will, he doesn't make empty promises, which is more than I can say for *some* employers."

That meant he probably wasn't holding anyone for ransom, then – unless his apparent wealth was a fraud of some sort.

"Would you know just how he intends to benefit humanity?"

Mad Bill shook his head. "I've no idea. I haven't met him, remember."

I considered this, remembering that Dr. Pierce had told me that Monsieur Boireau was very interested in the Lost City of the Mirage. Did he have some scheme to use the Lost City's secrets for some great purpose? Was he abducting scientists to aid in this mysterious endeavor?

That did fit together – but why was it necessary to *abduct* anyone, rather than just hiring them? Why had he not made his plans public?

The simplest way to pursue an answer, of course, would be to simply *ask* him. Accordingly, when Mad Bill and I had finished our meal and spent an additional half-hour in happy conversation, I turned my footsteps toward the Hotel Brunswick.

I had planned to leave a message at the front desk, as Mr. de la Rue had suggested, but that proved unnecessary, as the gentleman himself was picking up a newspaper there as I entered the lobby. I cannot say which of us recognized the other first; it was as close to simultaneous as one could ask.

"Mr. Derringer!" he called, as he tucked the paper under his arm and strode toward me. "What a pleasure to see you again!"

"Mr. de la Rue," I replied. "I have come to take your employer up on his offer."

"Excellent!" He held out his hand, and I shook it, albeit a trifle reluctantly. "When can you be available for an interview?"

"My schedule is quite open, at present, and I would be happy to meet with him at his earliest convenience."

"And where would you like to meet?"

I gestured toward two nearby chairs. "Why not here?"

De la Rue's smile vanished. "No, I'm afraid we must insist on somewhere private. My employer has enemies and does not like to appear in public places."

"Well, where would suit him, then?"

"He maintains an office on Hudson Street; would that be convenient?"

I did not know where Hudson Street was, as I was not really very familiar with the city as yet, but I was sure I could find it. "And when can we meet? This evening, perhaps?"

"I'm afraid he is not in the city at the moment, but he can be here by tomorrow afternoon – shall we say two o'clock?"

"I think that would be acceptable."

"Excellent!" He pulled out a pen and a small notebook. "Let me write down the address."

He did so, and handed me the slip of paper. I glanced at it, then tucked it in my pocket. "Until tomorrow, then," I said, tipping my hat.

With that we took our leave of one another. I do not know

where Mr. de la Rue went; I considered the possibility of following him surreptitiously, but under the circumstances, where he was watching me depart, I did not see a practical way to attempt it. When I left the Brunswick he was standing in the lobby, looking through the newspaper he had just acquired.

For myself, I had no shortage of things to do in New York that had nothing to do with my current investigation. I visited a few shops, stopped in at the headquarters of the Order of Theseus to take the next steps toward formally joining that organization, got supper at a pleasant little restaurant, and finally returned to the Robertson Hotel, where I wrote brief letters to Betsy and to my mother before retiring.

I did not go into any great detail about my findings; I wrote mostly to let them know I was still well.

And on the morrow I returned first to the Pierce Archives to refresh my memory on matters pertaining to the missing scientists and the Lost City – since I had already met with Mr. de la Rue I did not bother to make any inquiries about Cape May. From there I made my way to Mad Bill's tavern for lunch, before engaging a hansom to take me to Hudson Street, which was, unsurprisingly, on the west side of the island, only a few blocks from the Hudson River, and of considerable length, so much so that I was mildly surprised I had not known of it. The address I had been given proved to be a small office building, well downtown, and the meeting was to take place in Room Four. I arrived at half past one, give or take, and rather than hurry in I decided to scout out the area, and see if I could spot Monsieur Boireau's arrival.

I was lounging in a doorway across the street, trying to appear a mere idler, when a formidable fellow in a black coat strode up to the building across the street, stopped at the front door, and looked attentively up and down the street.

Was this Monsieur Boireau? I did not reveal myself yet.

Then *another* large man in a black coat, this one with a

beard halfway down his chest, approached from the other direction; he nodded to the first and took up a position beside him. They continued to keep a watchful eye on their surroundings, paying particular attention to male pedestrians; they both glanced in my direction, exchanged a few words, and then apparently dismissed me – though every so often their gaze would return to me briefly.

I took out my new pocket watch, which I had bought the day before and set that morning, and noted that there were still ten minutes to go until the appointed hour.

Finally, *three* men came marching down the sidewalk from the north, two more of the large, muscular sort flanking a much smaller but better-dressed individual. All five of these people gathered for a brief colloquy at the door of the building, and then went inside, the smaller man surrounded by the other four.

You have probably made the same guess I did – that the four large men were bodyguards, and the smaller fellow was Monsieur Boireau. This was, in fact, the case, or nearly so – I later learned that three were bodyguards and the fourth Monsieur Boireau's secretary, who may well have doubled for another bodyguard.

As they were entering the building one of them paused and looked back at me. He stared at me for a few seconds, and then followed his companions.

I supposed I had been spotted; well, I saw no real harm in that. I straightened up, adjusted my hat, and crossed the street.

Room Four was upstairs, alongside the staircase; I found it easily enough. I would have found it readily, I think, even without the bodyguard standing by the door, but his presence made it even simpler.

As I approached he said, "Mr. Derringer?"

"I'm Tom Derringer," I acknowledged.

"Monsieur Boireau is expecting you." He opened the door, and stepped aside.

I entered the room cautiously, unsure what to expect. What I found was Monsieur Boireau seated behind a desk, a bodyguard on either side, while the last of his four companions was sitting in a chair by the window. The walls were lined with bookshelves and file cabinets, and in general it looked very much like any other office. There were three other chairs available; I started toward the armchair nearest the desk, then looked inquiringly at my host.

"Please, Mr. Derringer, make yourself comfortable," he said, gesturing at the chair. He spoke with only a slight French accent. Long ago, one of my tutors had tried to teach me to distinguish one French accent from another; I had never mastered that particular skill. I seem to lack the ear for it. If I had been forced to guess, though, I would have said he was from Paris, or somewhere near it, or at any rate not one of the more distinctive outlying regions.

I noticed that he did not offer his hand.

I removed my hat and settled myself. "Mr. Boireau, I presume?"

"I am Sebastien Boireau," he said. Then he glanced at the man by the window, who nodded.

"You offered to pay me for a few hours of my time," I said. "I am here to take you up on that."

"Indeed." He reached inside his jacket and brought out a purse, then counted out five gold eagles, which he set upon the desk.

I did not reach for them, since I had not yet earned them. "Ask your questions then, M'sieu."

He winced at my pronunciation, and I decided not to attempt any further French. I could read the language, at least to some extent, but my ability to speak it was much more limited.

"Are you armed?" he asked.

I was not, having deliberately left my pistol at my hotel, and said so, adding, "I had thought this was to be a friendly conversation." I looked meaningfully at his bodyguards.

He raised one hand and waved, and the two behind the desk marched out of the room, closing the door behind them. The man by the window remained. I looked at him.

"Mr. Cathcart is my aide," Monsieur Boireau said. "My secretary."

"I see. Will Mr. de la Rue be joining us?"

"No, I'm afraid he is attending to other duties at present.

I nodded. "Then ask me whatever questions you have."

He nodded. "Then let us go to it. Have you, Mr. Derringer, ever seen the Lost City of the Mirage?"

"Only in drawings and photographs."

"You have not, personally, been near it?"

"I have not."

"You had dealings with a man named Hezekiah McKee?"

"I did, yes."

"Could you tell me about that? In as much detail as possible, please."

I did not take him literally, but I began, "I read reports of a mysterious object having been seen in the skies above the Arizona Territory, and that caught my interest. It seemed to me that the only way to properly investigate a flying object would be aboard a flying machine of my own, so I began making inquiries..."

He listened intently and did not interrupt as I described my purchase of the Vanderhart Aeronavigator, my flight south from Flagstaff, my long pursuit of Reverend McKee's aluminum airship, and the events that followed upon finally locating it.

That took perhaps an hour; after all, he had asked for as much detail as possible. I did not actually oblige him in this, however; I was careful to make as little mention of Miss Vanderhart as I could. I did not mention that it had been she who piloted the Aeronavigator, she who improvised the breathing apparatus we used to get aboard McKee's vessel, and she who actually shot McKee. I did not want him to decide that abducting *her* might be a good idea.

When I had finished with our return to New York, there was a moment of silence; he sat back in his chair, fingers steepled before his chin. Then he sat up again, and asked, "And what did Reverend McKee or any of his crewmen tell you about this metal he had taken from the Lost City? Did they say how it had been used in the City?"

This was not quite the line of questioning I had expected, and I struggled to recall whatever I might have heard.

"I think I was told that it had been used for lampposts, fences, and railings, but I cannot promise my memory is correct."

"Lampposts – what of wire?"

"I do not recall any mention of wire. I'm not even sure aluminum wire is possible."

"And can you be sure this metal was, in fact, aluminum, and not something more exotic?"

I blinked in surprise. "I have not heard anyone question it before," I said. "I am not sure I heard anyone say definitively that it *was* aluminum, but it certainly matched every description of aluminum I have encountered, and when I spoke to McKee's crewmen about its possible value, no one suggested that it was anything other than aluminum. At least two other well-educated people I spoke with, one of them a trained engineer, believed it to be aluminum."

"Hmm." Monsieur Boireau frowned, and asked, "Did Reverend McKee's vessel display any unusual electrical equipment?"

"There were Edison lamps in use throughout."

"Could you determine whether they were in any way out of the ordinary?"

"Other than being Edison lamps in the wilds of southern Mexico?"

"Yes. Were they in aluminum cases, perhaps?"

"I am not intimately familiar with Edison lamps, sir, but I saw nothing remarkable about these. I saw no aluminum cases or other aluminum elements; aluminum had been used to build the airship's frame, and for some of the decks and bulkheads, but nowhere else that I observed."

"Aluminum aside for the present, there were no unusual navigational instruments, or signaling devices?"

"Not that I noticed, but I was never permitted access to the ship's controls, and I possess no particular expertise in navigation equipment."

"You didn't explore the wreckage after you brought it down?"

"I did not. We made our way directly to Belize Town."

"Has anyone else investigated the downed vessel?"

"Not to my certain knowledge, but I would guess someone has."

"Can you provide me with its exact location?"

"Exact? I am afraid not. Approximate, yes, but I had neither map nor compass; we took our bearings from the sun in making our way south."

He pursed his lips. "I will want you to give me your best guess. For now, though, I have more questions."

And he continued, for quite some time.

Chapter Six

My Search Begins

In time, Monsieur Boireau's questions came to an end. He shook my hand, paid me the promised fee, and dismissed me.

I had expected to be asked for every detail I might have of Hezekiah McKee's visit to the Lost City, and of course, I did not have many – what little I knew had come from one long-ago conversation with Gerhardt von Düssel. McKee himself had told me nothing during our brief confrontation, nor had the subject come up in any other discussions during my stay aboard his airship. I had supposed that Monsieur Boireau's primary interest would be in determining how he might locate the Lost City, and what he might hope to find there, but instead he had been focused entirely on what McKee had brought *out* of the City, and what had become of it. He seemed to think it highly probable that McKee had scavenged electrical devices from the mysterious ruins and had used these devices aboard his airship. He seemed quite disappointed that I knew of nothing McKee might have retrieved other than the massive quantities of aluminum he had used to construct the Skymaster.

He had had no questions at all about the City itself, but only about the aluminum and any electrical devices I might have seen or inferred aboard McKee's airship. Since I had not, in fact, seen anything out of the ordinary, I think the interview had been frustrating for him, but he had remained polite throughout and had not voiced any displeasure at my answers.

With the assistance of a map he drew from a drawer of his

desk I had provided him with my best guess as to just where McKee's Skymaster had gone down, and he had considered that thoughtfully before resuming his questions.

As I had said to Tobias Arbuthnot, one sometimes learns more from being questioned than one reveals. I was beginning to make sense of the connections among the missing scientists and adventurers – assuming, of course, that Monsieur Boireau was in fact involved in them, as I was now more certain than ever was the case. It seemed to me that he was not only obsessed with the Lost City of the Mirage, but that he believed many of the mysterious artifacts that had been seen there to be electrical devices of one sort or another. He clearly wanted to obtain some of these devices, or perhaps duplicate them based on the descriptions, photographs, and fragments that various explorers had brought back from the City. He had, I theorized, recruited these men to aid him in his efforts.

But why had they not been sent safely home again after they were questioned? Where were they now? He had not tried to take *me* captive, nor to kill me; I was free and walking up Hudson Street. His various guards had made no attempt to impede my departure.

I glanced back at the guards, still lounging by the door. They did not seem to be paying me any particular attention.

Perhaps Monsieur Boireau did not consider me to be of any further use after today's conversation.

Or perhaps his men would come after me later; after all, Mrs. Vanderhart's account had said that her husband and Mr. de la Rue had spoken for some time, on apparently friendly terms, and that the kidnapping had only occurred afterward. That was a worrisome possibility. I wondered if perhaps it would be unwise to return to the Robertson Hotel. I tried to remember whether I had ever said where I was staying to either de la Rue or Boireau; I did not think I had, but was not absolutely certain. And of course, I had not deliberately kept it secret from others I had spoken with, such as Tobias Arbuthnot or Mad Bill; I had almost certainly mentioned it to Toby.

I had been planning to stay in New York for another few days, but I began to reconsider. I knew I might be giving in to irrational suspicion, but an excess of caution would do me no harm.

I did return to the Robertson, but only long enough to pack my things, check out of my room, and settle my bill. I then proceeded to the station to catch a train out of the city.

The question, of course, was where I was to go. I had considered that as I packed, and as I walked. If I was indeed to be a target of the kidnapper, whether it was Boireau, de la Rue, or someone else, I did not want to go anywhere he would expect to find me, nor anywhere that my friends or other innocents might be endangered. I certainly was not going home; my mother had always been careful to keep its location, if not actually secret, at least not widely known, and leading pursuers there would be a very bad idea. Nor would I return to New Brunswick, where my presence might endanger Betsy and her family.

Furthermore, I wanted to continue my investigation, and a certain detail had been troubling me intermittently since I first read Mr. de la Rue's letter in Tobias Arbuthnot's office. He had given his address as General Delivery, Cape May, New Jersey.

What was he doing in Cape May? Was he hiding the various missing men somewhere in that vicinity?

Accordingly, after I left the Robertson Hotel I boarded a Philadelphia & Reading train for Camden, where I could change for Cape May.

I took my supper in Camden and arrived in Cape May quite late in the evening; fortunately it was early enough in the year that I had no trouble getting a room at the Hotel Chalfonte, on Howard Street – an absolutely lovely place built in a fine southern style. In the summer I have no doubt the place would have been jammed with happy families enjoying seaside vacations, with no room for a late arrival, but the weather had not yet warmed enough to make the Atlantic beaches attractive. In fact, a cold wind was blowing, and clouds overhead threatened rain.

I slept well and ate a fine breakfast at my hotel. When I had finished I asked at the front desk for directions to the post office, which proved to be just half a dozen blocks away. Had the weather been better, it would probably have been a delightful stroll, but the threatened rain had arrived in the night and was miserably steady. Nor had the temperature risen appreciably. I kept my collar up and my coat pulled tight while I hurried through the rain-swept streets.

At the post office, which fortunately was not busy, I explained my quest, at least in part; I said I was looking for Leopold de la Rue, and I knew he lived in Cape May, but had no street address for him.

"I'm afraid it's not our business to keep track of our general delivery customers," the clerk replied.

"Do you know him, though?" I asked.

"I wouldn't go that far. I would suppose I've met him a time or two."

"Does Cape May have home delivery? I would have thought it was of a size to provide it."

He was visibly offended. "Of course we do! But only in town; we don't try to find every fisherman and hermit north of the harbor. They come into town for their mail."

"I wouldn't have thought Mr. de la Rue to be a fisherman or a hermit."

"I didn't say he was. Some people just prefer to come here to fetch their mail."

"So you don't have any idea where I might find him?"

"No, sir, I do not."

While that was hardly the answer I had hoped for, it was all I could have reasonably expected. "Well, thank you for your time, sir," I said, tipping my hat. "I wish you a good day."

I left the post office and stood for a moment on the street corner at the intersection of Washington and Franklin, huddling against the rain and trying to decide on my next move. The weather was quite discouraging; I had thought I might do some exploring, perhaps make some inquiries at the various hotels and eating establishments, but that prospect was far from appealing.

About all I knew was that de la Rue lived somewhere near enough to get his mail here, but probably not in Cape May proper. He surely would not bother coming here if Atlantic City was closer, but that still left a good bit of territory to consider.

This assumed that he actually *had* a permanent lodging in the area and did not move from place to place.

How did Sebastien Boireau fit into this? Mr. de la Rue worked for him, and Boireau had not been in New York City on Wednesday; might he have been somewhere in the wilds of southern New Jersey?

I really had no solid evidence of that; it might be that de la Rue came here on his own business, while Boireau could have been upstate, or in Connecticut or Pennsylvania, or some other part of New Jersey entirely.

It was frustrating. I decided to return to my hotel and consider the situation somewhere dry.

Since I had little else productive to occupy my time, I wired my mother and Miss Vanderhart to assure them I was alive and well and that I might be making some progress in my investigation. After that I retired to one of the hotel lounges with the day's newspapers.

There were no reports of further disappearances, nor had any of the missing been located – at least, not that had been reported in the popular press.

When I could no longer force myself to read any further I returned to the hotel lobby, where I took a seat near the windows and gazed resentfully out at the rain, trying to devise a useful course of action.

"Not exactly a good day for a stroll on the beach, is it?" someone asked. I looked up to find a stranger standing at my shoulder.

"No, it certainly is not," I agreed.

"Seems as if it might be letting up,"

"I hope it does."

"Of course, it's still pretty cold."

"Well, maybe if the sun comes out, that will improve."

"Maybe." He looked down at me and held out a hand. "I'm George Moss. I work in real estate here in town."

"Tom Derringer," I said, shaking his hand. "Just visiting."

"Haven't noticed you around; have you been in town long?"

"No, I only got in last night."

"Staying long?"

"I don't really know. I was looking for someone, but it seems the address I had was wrong – or rather, doesn't exist."

"Oh, now that's awkward! Who were you looking for?"

"A Mr. Leopold de la Rue."

Mr. Moss considered that for a moment, then shook his head. "Don't believe I know him. Who is he?"

"An acquaintance of my father-in-law's," I said, hoping Betsy would forgive me for implying a relationship that I hoped to have one day, but that did not, as yet, exist. "I'm supposed to arrange a meeting."

"Well, who is this de la Rue? A lawyer?"

"No, I...I don't really know. I think he might be involved in some sort of scientific research."

Mr. Moss frowned. "Not a lot of *that* going on around here! Unless that's what those people are doing out on Wildwood Island."

I blinked. "I'm sorry?"

He looked around, found a chair, pulled it over near my own, and sat down. "Wildwood Island. It's a... well, really, it's not much more than a big sandbar with some marshy bits, just to the northeast. Virtually uninhabited. And then a little over a year ago someone started buying it up, and chasing off the few people who *had* been living there. Which was a good thing for *me*, because some of them came looking for new homes. I did mention I was in real estate?"

"You did, yes. If you'll forgive me for my bluntness, is that why you're chatting up strangers in hotel lobbies?"

He smiled, clearly not taking offense. "Clever lad! It is *precisely* why. You'd be surprised how many of our visitors decide they would like a more permanent foothold here on the Cape."

"I'm afraid you're wasting your time with me, then."

"Ah, but look around – do you see any better prospects?" A wave of his arm took in the entirety of the lobby, which was indeed very sparsely inhabited. "And weather like this is hardly going to encourage sales, in any case."

"Well, I certainly don't mind the company," I said. "Now, what was this you were saying about this Wide Wood Island?"

"Wildwood," he corrected me. "Yes, some Frenchman bought up the whole island last year. His name wasn't de la Rue, I don't remember it exactly, but that name being French it brought him to mind, and for all I know he wanted it so he could research the local shellfish or something."

I felt a growing excitement. "Could his name have been Boireau, perhaps?

"No, I don't think that was it, either – though I might have heard that name somewhere. How's it spelled? These French names..."

I spelled it.

"Boyrio?"

"Boireau," I corrected – not that my own pronunciation would have passed muster in Paris.

"Well, that wasn't the buyer's name, though I might have

heard this Bwarro mentioned." He shook his head. "Or maybe I'm just imagining it. Who's this Bwarro, then?" He pronounced the name to rhyme with "barrow," but I saw no point in correcting him.

"I am given to understand that Mr. de la Rue, the man I'm looking for, works for him."

"I suppose there just might be some connection, then."

"There might, at that." I would, I decided, take a look at Wildwood Island at the first opportunity.

But that was not going to be that morning, in the rain. "I take it you try to do what you can to promote the local enterprises?"

"I do, yes. Was there something I could help you with?"

"I was wondering about where the best luncheon might be found. And is there anything you would particularly recommend I see while I'm here?"

That was enough to launch a lengthy description of the wonders of Cape May, from restaurants to candy shops and artists' ateliers, with much commentary on how splendidly it had recovered and rebuilt after the disastrous fire that had laid waste to most of the city five or six years ago. Everything, I was assured, was now thoroughly modern and up to date.

I listened, though not very attentively. I was far more interested in learning who had bought up this mysterious island to the north than I was in the delights of Cape May itself, and I was intensely curious as to how he might be related (if at all) to Monsieur Boireau and Mr. de la Rue. I intended to find out.

But not, I thought as I glanced out the window, until the rain stopped.

Chapter Seven

An Astonishing Discovery

To my pleased surprise, the clouds broke and the sun emerged shortly after midday. After bidding Mr. Moss farewell, I had discussed Wildwood Island with the desk clerk.

He seemed unable imagine why anyone would want to go there. "I assure you, Mr. Derringer, you'll find much nicer beaches right here in town," he said. "And if you're following in Mr. Audubon's footsteps and looking for birds, I don't think you'll find any on Wildwood that you won't see in more accessible places."

"Is the island difficult to reach, then?"

"Well, yes, sir – it's an *island*. There are no bridges or ferries, and it's separated from the mainland by a string of lakes and lagoons, and about a mile of marshland. To the best of my knowledge, it doesn't have a proper landing anywhere. That's why no one lives there."

"I had heard that there *were* a few residents."

"Well, there were a *few*, but the new owner chased them away last year. I don't think a living soul has set foot there in months."

Meeting Mr. Moss had initially seemed a stroke of good fortune, but now I was beginning to wonder whether it had been fortunate after all. Any investigation of Wildwood Island might prove to be a wild goose chase.

But on the other hand – where better to hide a dozen

kidnapped scientists than on a desert island off the New Jersey coast?

I had not, until that very day, realized there *were* desert islands off the New Jersey coast. I wondered how long it would be before the growing demand for living space and seaside resorts brought development to Wildwood – not long, I guessed.

For now, though, it was fairly inaccessible. Someday a bridge or causeway might be built, or ferries put into operation, but as yet such amenities were unavailable.

"Can one hire a boat here in town?"

"Well, of *course* you can! Good heavens, sir, what sort of a seaside resort would we be if we had no boats for charter? Though I'm not sure how many are operating this early in the year. I'm afraid I can't name a specific one, but if you go down to the harbor I'm sure you'll find signs advertising them."

"And how do I get to the harbor?"

"You go out to Columbia Avenue... Here, I think I had better write it out for you."

And thus, not long after lunch and only minutes after the sun had finally burst through the skies, I found myself bound for the harbor, with a leather bag on my shoulder and poorly written but functional directions on a scrap of hotel stationery in my hand. The bag held an assortment of items I thought might prove useful, including my Colt revolver and assorted tools.

The journey was a walk of roughly a mile and a half; despite the recent rain the streets were well drained and not particularly muddy, and I arrived without incident.

As the clerk had said, many of the waterfront businesses had not yet opened for the season, but I wandered along the water's edge until I spotted a sign advertising boat rentals. I climbed down the steps to the little shed that served as an office and inquired of the young man I found there as to what they had on offer.

He had plainly been caught off guard by my arrival, but

dropped his feet from the front of an unlit stove, sat up, and asked what I might be interested in.

I explained that I wanted to visit Wildwood Island.

He seemed at first to be inclined to ask why I would want to visit such a desolate place, but he caught himself before actually saying as much. Instead he asked, "Just you, sir?"

"Just me."

"Would you want to hire a crew, or would you be sailing it yourself?"

About three years earlier I had taken boats out on Lake Oneida and Lake George a few times and learned the basics of handling them from an old seaman by the name of John Brown – no relation, he assured me, to the famous abolitionist rabble rouser. He had also assured me that the placid lakes of my home state were nothing like the wild Atlantic, and while I suspected him of exaggeration and thought the sea looked fairly calm that day, I saw no point in putting what I remembered of his teachings to the test. Courtesy of Monsieur Boireau, I had sufficient funds in my pocket to cover the cost of hiring professionals.

"I think I'd prefer to hire a sailor," I said.

"But it's just you, no other passengers?"

"That's right."

"Then it's probably not worth firing up the steamer. Are you comfortable with a small sailboat?"

I assured him that I was, and half an hour later his brother Albert and I were sailing up the harbor in a tidy little craft – I have no idea just what sort she was, but she was fore-and-aft rigged, and perhaps thirty feet from stem to stern, with the name *Eliza Anne* blazoned across the transom. Albert seemed to have no problem in handling her by himself.

We were scarcely out of the town harbor when I saw that the shore to the left had become wild marshland, apparently uninhabited. I remarked upon this.

"Lot of that around here," Albert replied. "If you're looking for good land to build on, you'll need to go around to the west side of the cape."

"I'm not looking for land," I replied. "I just want to get a good look at Wildwood. I've heard some rumors about it."

"Rumors?" He shook his head. "It's an island. It's got some better land than those marshes, and it has some good beaches, if there were an easy way to get to them. I've heard of folks sailing up there for picnics, or a little romance away from the crowds, but I wouldn't call those rumors."

"How far is it?" I had not had a chance to look at a map.

He looked startled and pointed out past the bow. "It's right there," he said.

I looked, but he clearly saw my lack of comprehension.

"On the left there's the marsh," he said, indicating with his finger. "And on the right, that's Sewell Point, with the Navy station. Ahead on the left is the entrance to Jarvis Sound, which they call the Thorofare, and ahead on the right is Cape May Inlet that takes you out to the Atlantic, and that land between them? That's Wildwood Island."

"So close!" I exclaimed.

"It's maybe two miles from the harbor waterfront. Not more than three."

"But no one's done anything with it? There aren't any bridges or ferries?"

He shrugged. "Not yet," he said. "The way things have been growing since the big fire, though, I wouldn't be surprised if someone put 'em in soon."

This reminded me of what I had seen in the newspapers and what Mr. Moss had told me. Half the city of Cape May had burned to the ground in the fall of 1878, and the rebuilt area was said to boast some of the finest architecture in the latest styles. I resolved to wander down into that part of town and take a look, should I find myself with time to spare. Perhaps that new construction had some connection with my investigations.

For now, though, I was more concerned with Wildwood. I watched it grow closer – a low rise topped with trees above a gravel beach, far rougher than the fine sands along Cape May's Atlantic shore.

Albert looked up at the sails, then turned his head to take in our location and judge the wind. "Did you want to actually *land* on the island?" he asked. "There aren't any docks, but I can bring us in close."

"I'm not sure," I admitted. "Not right on this end, certainly."

Albert considered this, then said, "Did you want to go up into Jarvis Sound, or out along the Atlantic beaches?"

It seemed to me that it would be much harder to hide something on the oceanic side of the island, where ships would pass by with some regularity. "Into the Sound, please."

Albert nodded, and pulled on a rope – or rather, remembering my nautical training, a sheet – to shift the sail. The boat heeled over onto the other tack, and we shifted our course to the north.

The channel between the island and the marsh was broad, so that navigating it was not challenging, but I did wonder how deep it was and how much water our little craft drew; I assumed there was a keel to counterbalance the sails, so that hitting bottom was a genuine risk. Albert seemed unconcerned, though, and he was, I assumed, quite familiar with these waters.

"That's Thorofare Island," he informed me, as I saw the channel splitting ahead. "I'll take the right–hand passage to keep us closer to Wildwood."

I nodded agreement, though the right–hand passage was far narrower than the left, and my concerns about the keel touching bottom had not lessened. I was putting my faith in Albert's experience and expertise.

That faith was not misplaced; we rounded Thorofare Island without incident and emerged into a broad expanse of open water that Albert identified as Jarvis Sound. This was surrounded on all sides by marsh, not merely on the west; it seemed that not *all* of Wildwood Island was solid ground.

I had no desire to attempt a landing there, so we proceeded northward, across the sound and through another channel into a second wide open area for which Albert had no distinct name – it was just more of Jarvis Sound, so far as he knew.

The island looked much more solid here, though.

I glanced back and observed that Cape May was no longer visible astern; there was no sign of human habitation to be seen, just the marshes to the west and the islands to east and south.

We continued past what Albert identified as Ephraim Island on our left, along the shore of Wildwood Island on our right, which, while no longer a marshy wasteland, still appeared quite desolate and uninhabited. The sound narrowed to a channel again, and then widened out, and split. Assuming that we were once again approaching a small island like Thorofare or Ephraim, I pointed to the headland between these two passages and asked, "What's *that* island?"

"Oh, that's Wildwood," he replied. "The channel's on the left; that on the right is Post Creek. It doesn't go anywhere." He was already turning our craft to port.

"A creek? You mean a stream?"

"Well, not really. There's no current or anything. It goes into a basin, where there's no other way out. It's all Wildwood."

"That's interesting," I said. The afternoon was wearing on, and the skies beginning to darken as the clouds gathered anew, but I was enjoying this excursion, even if the results had as yet been disappointing. I was in no hurry to end it. "Let's take a look at this basin."

Albert looked inclined to argue, but I added, "I'm paying by the hour, am I not?"

He frowned, but brought the bow back to starboard. He adjusted the sails, as the channel was rather narrow, but we sailed through it without mishap. Albert kept us in the center, and frequently glanced over the side, as if concerned about the depth of the water beneath our keel.

Just as he had said, we emerged into an enclosed lake or basin; most of the visible shoreline was marshy, and all in all it was not a particularly attractive place.

The clouds above us were definitely thickening; to the west the sun was only visible as a bright spot in the overcast. Albert looked up, obviously uncomfortable with the threatening weather and shallow water.

I could understand his attitude. He had not wanted to detour into this unprepossessing place, and I was sure that he did not want to be trapped here should a sudden storm blow up from the west; it might be impossible to make it back through the passage should a strong wind be blowing against us. I started to say that we could turn back, when something caught my eye – a sparkle on the shore to the southeast. "What's that?" I asked.

"What's what?" he responded.

"Over there," I said, pointing.

"I don't see any..." he began.

I pointed again. "*There.*"

There was a light, one that did not look natural, at the top of an odd little spire, just visible behind a line of trees. What's more, now that my attention was drawn to that area, I could see two other spires, one on either side of the one that held that curious lamp, and other unfamiliar structures.

"Is there a lighthouse on the island?" I asked .

"Nope," he said. He was staring, now, just as I was.

That light, I thought, looked rather like an Edison lamp – a very large one, if it was as far away as it appeared to be. It did not have the glaring intensity of a carbon arc lamp, nor the blue tinge of a gas flame, and the color was not right for kerosene or whale oil.

"That wasn't there before," he said.

"When was the last time you were here?"

"Ah... last August?"

"Well, that's time for someone to have built that," I said. "Take us closer."

"To that light?"

"Yes, to that light! I'm fairly sure that light is exactly what I came looking for!"

I had little doubt that the glow was created by electricity. I did not know the exact method, as I had never seen an Edison incandescent that size, but neither did it resemble any sort of ordinary flame. And most of the missing scientists – not all, but most – had been known for working with electricity.

Just then there was a sudden blue-white flash, just for an instant, somewhere below the spires. I had no idea what it was, but it clearly deserved further investigation.

"What was *that?*" Albert exclaimed.

"I don't know, but I intend to find out," I replied. "Bring us into shore."

"I don't... I don't think it's safe," Albert said.

"I don't know that it is, but I'm pretty sure this place is what I came here to find."

"The water's too shallow. We'll run aground."

"Well, take us as close as you dare!"

He reluctantly obeyed, but it was quickly evident that Albert was not as daring a young man as I might have hoped. He would not take us nearer than a hundred yards or more from shore. When I urged him to continue, he protested that the water here was not merely shallow but full of snags, and he would not risk damaging his brother's boat.

"It can't be that bad," I said. "Look, there's a boat dock with a boat tied up!"

There was, in fact, such a dock, angling out from the shore. The boat appeared to be a steamer, only a little larger than our own vessel. They had been largely hidden by low trees until we made our approach.

"The channel's not marked," Albert insisted.

"Perhaps it doesn't need to be! Can't you see the clear water leading to it?"

"That dock's probably private property. I don't want to be shot for trespassing."

I somehow suspected that the mysterious flash had more to do with his reservations than any concerns about trespassing. Exasperated, I decided that I did not need to be limited by Albert's caution; that boat at the pier meant I would not be stranded, that there were other ways of reaching the mainland besides the *Eliza Anne*.

"Fine," I said. "Hold her steady." Then I took off my hat and coat, emptied several useful items from my pockets, and wrapped them in an oiled canvas rag. I stuffed that bundle into my leather shoulder bag, alongside the supplies already there. I removed my shoes and socks and added them to the collection.

Albert had watched in confused surprise as I did this. At last I turned to him and said, "I am going ashore. Would you please return my hat and coat to my hotel? I'm staying at the Chalfonte."

"You...what?"

"I'm going ashore, even if you aren't. In case you did not get my name, it's Derringer, Tom Derringer. If the hotel clerk asks, I left the clothes in your boat by accident, you have no idea where I've gone, but you're sure I'll come back eventually."

"Mr. Derringer, you don't know what's over there!"

"Albert, I'm a professional adventurer. I intend to *find out* what's over there."

"You're an *adventurer*? I thought you were a tourist!"

"I preferred not to announce my occupation." I fished out a handful of silver and counted out what I thought I owed, then added a dollar. "That should cover my bill, I believe – if not, we can settle up when I get back to Cape May. Now, give me a hand getting myself over the gunwale, if you would be so kind."

Albert did not offer his hand. Instead he asked, "Mr. Derringer, how will you get *back*?"

"If no other opportunity presents itself, I will swim. The inlet did not appear impossible to cross by such means."

He looked sincerely distressed. "Mr. Derringer, it's not so much the distance. You're right, the narrowest part of the inlet is only maybe three hundred yards across, and maybe you can swim that far, but the currents can be fierce, and the water is *cold*. It doesn't really warm up here until July. I don't think you should risk it."

I started to protest, then stopped. I knew that foolish pride and overconfidence had cost many an adventurer his life. "All right, then, what would you suggest? Do you want to wait here?"

"How long will you be?"

"I don't know. It might be hours."

"I can't just stay here indefinitely! Not with those people over there, and with it getting dark."

"Do you have an alternative to offer?"

"I could come back first thing in the morning and look for you."

That was a generous offer. I nodded. "I will do my best to be on the beach at the southern end of the island, then – you did say there are beaches on the ocean side?"

"Yes, there are."

"The morning light should make it easier to spot me on the eastern side, I should think."

"I guess so."

"And of course, whether we find one another or not, I will pay you for your time." I fished out more coins. "Consider this a down payment."

He accepted the money. "I'll keep your coat and hat with me. But are you really sure you want to do this?"

"Quite sure. Now, give me a hand."

He obliged, and watched as I slid into the water. Then he handed me my bag, and I slung it on my shoulder before releasing my hold on the *Eliza Anne*.

The water was far colder than I had expected, vindicating Albert's concern, but I did not have far to go; I suppressed my shivering as best I could and set out for shore – swimming at first, but quickly discovering after I had gone no more than a dozen yards that the water was shallow enough that I could wade. As well as being correct about the temperature of the water, Albert had not been wrong to fear running aground. As I stood upright I turned, and waved to him.

He was already setting sail. He took just one look back at me, then swung his little craft over on the port tack and headed away.

I did not bother to watch him go. Instead I turned and slogged toward shore, trying not to splash too loudly.

Chapter Eight

The Electrical Empire

As soon as I was out of the sea I paused, shivering, and squeezed as much water as I could out of my clothes. I dried my feet as best I could with a cloth from my bag, then put my shoes back on; my fingers were unsteady, but at last I managed to tie the laces. I stood up and looked around. I was still trembling with cold, but the chill was starting to pass now that I was once again on land.

I was perhaps fifty yards west of the pier, and a hundred yards or so from the nearest of those three little spires. Peering out across the water I could not see Albert or the *Eliza Anne*, but whether that was because he had successfully departed the area, or because they were lost in the gathering gloom, I could not be entirely sure.

I looked along the shore and realized the only path in sight led from the dock up toward the spires; the rest of the shoreline was still, so far as I could see, in a completely natural state, undisturbed by any human activity. Only a single boat was tied up to the dock, the little steamer I had seen from the *Eliza Anne*, and the area was deserted, so far as I could see, except for a figure seated on the deck of the steamer, who appeared to be napping – his head was bowed, his arms folded across his chest.

If there were any guards or fences they were not in sight, a fact that made me doubt my initial assumption that this was where the missing scientists were being held. Still, those spires definitely seemed to be worth investigating, and *something* up there had caused that flash.

A year or two earlier I might have simply made my way to the boat dock and asked the dozing boatman a few questions, but my experiences in Mexico and the Far West, and Betsy's comments on my behavior, had made me more cautious. Instead I headed inland, up the slope, making my way through the weeds and switchgrass.

I was still shivering; the water had been *very* cold, and despite my efforts my clothes were still wet. I doubted I was in any real danger of hypothermia, but I still hoped to get out of the wind and into someplace warm. I wondered whether I had been too hasty in leaving my coat with Albert.

As I passed the first line of trees I got a better look at the structures and stopped to stare.

In addition to the three spires I had seen before there were several other structures rising above a massive windowless gray wall, a wall perhaps twenty feet high and easily a hundred yards or more in length. The wall's gray color had allowed it to blend into the background of clouds when I was farther away.

If this was not my intended destination, it was still obviously something worth investigation, and I thought it very probable that the missing scientists, including Professor Vanderhart, were beyond that wall.

There was no obvious way to gain entrance. I saw no doorways or gates.

But I also saw no guards or patrols, and I decided I could safely take a closer look. I had passed most of the weeds, and the ground before me was mostly sand, punctuated with hummocks of grass of one sort or another, so my approach was not difficult. I gave some thought to trying to hide my tracks, but concluded it was not worth the effort.

The wall, I saw, was not vertical; it sloped away from me, toward whatever was on the other side. That, I thought, might prove convenient; it would make it easier to scale, should I need to do so.

A short walk brought me to the wall's base, where I could look it over. I had already observed that it was painted a singularly unattractive drab gray, and at first I thought it might be metal or concrete, but a closer inspection confirmed it was merely wood. There were no openings of any sort on the side I could see; the seams between the wooden beams had been filled and painted over. It was, in fact, as close to featureless as human industry could contrive. I turned to my right and continued walking, to see what might be around the corner.

And that was simply another wall, equal in height and length, and just as featureless. I hesitated, unsure whether to double back toward the shore, or proceed around the next side of the enclosure. In the end I decided to continue. I marched on along the sands and discovered that from this vantage I could see and even hear the Atlantic a few hundred yards to the southeast, white waves rolling in and breaking on sandy beaches. Apparently Wildwood Island was not particularly wide at this point. I also thought I saw other structures in the distance, to the south, though I could not tell, through the scrubby brush and the gathering gloom, whether they were mere storage sheds or something more interesting. I estimated that there were enough to constitute a good–sized village. I decided they might merit further investigation, once I had completed my study of the main enclosure.

And at the next corner, I found the third side of the wall – the easternmost, if I had not lost my bearings – to be just as blank and boring as the first two, though a crude road did cut through the sand alongside its entire length. The road showed signs of recent use.

The fourth, northerly face of the square was where I finally found something of interest. Midway along the wall was a sort of gatehouse where the road originated, perhaps fifteen feet high rather than the full height of the wall, complete with men I took to be sentries atop it.

The sentries, if that was what they were, were not particularly alert, though; rather than standing at attention they were seated comfortably, leaning back against the wall, and appeared to be chatting idly. I could hear their voices, even over the sound of the distant surf, but I could not make out their words. They were clearly not expecting any unfriendly visitors.

Having observed the entire perimeter, I retreated to the eastern side and considered the wall. I had not brought any actual climbing equipment in my bag – one cannot prepare for *every* eventuality – but I had a few assorted knives and spikes, and I thought that I ought to be able to drive them into one of the painted–over seams and scale the barrier thereby. The walk around the structure had warmed my blood, and my clothes had largely dried, so I was no longer shivering, and I thought such a climb well within my abilities.

I glanced up and down the road and decided this was not the right place to attempt entry. Someone might come along at any minute. I retraced my steps further, to roughly the midpoint of the south side, and found a spot I thought would be less visible than most.

The next question was whether I should make the attempt immediately, or wait until dark, to reduce the chance of being seen. The sun was on the western horizon, and the sky was now heavily overcast, so it would not be so very long until dark...

But then lights began to shine over the top of the wall – first just one, then another, and another. Clearly, I could not expect the night to provide any cover unless I waited for those lights to go out again, and I had no assurance that they would be extinguished before dawn.

That removed any reason for hesitation. I slung my bag on my shoulder once again, then plunged a Bowie knife deep into one of the seams a foot above my head, and used it to pull myself upward as I walked up the slope. Without that grip I would have slipped or fallen back, but with the knife's support I was able to hold on until I could sink another blade perhaps three feet higher.

That second knife was not as secure as the first, but the slope of the wall was of considerable assistance; I did not need to place my entire weight on the knives, or any substantial portion of it, but only required them to keep me from slipping back down.

I repositioned the Bowie knife and heaved myself up. In the next position, though, I could not get the blade to stay secure in the seam, and instead drove it, as hard as I could, into the wood itself.

Fortunately, the wall was not built of oak or ironwood or anything of that sort, and I was able to drive the blade's point an inch or more into the wood. I added a third knife nearby, just in case – that was the last knife I had that was big enough to be practical for this purpose – and continued my climb, relocating the knives as necessary.

It was not an especially difficult feat, and it did not take me long to reach the top. I had half expected to find a rampart, with guards patrolling, but instead I discovered that the wall was perhaps a foot thick and capped with ordinary tin.

When I heaved my head and shoulders above that strip of tin and saw what lay beyond, though, it was nothing I had anticipated. The enclosure was full of buildings – towers, domes, and arches, many of them thirty or forty feet high, all jammed close together. I located the three spires I had seen from the water; they were among the tallest structures.

Between the buildings were walkways, narrow streets, and steel tracks. Wires were strung everywhere and were clearly in use, as sparks showered every so often from their various connections. The place was far from silent; there was a constant low hum punctuated with cracklings and hisses. Several men were going about their business along the streets and walkways –

some in ordinary street clothes, others in workmen's overalls, and still others in laboratory coats. There were also a few who seemed to be standing guard at one door or another; these all wore dark jackets and hats of a vaguely military appearance, reminiscent of the kepi hats Union troops had worn of old. Most of the men were on foot, but a few were riding carts that ran on those steel tracks, wheels squealing and spitting sparks whenever they took a sharp curve.

I saw no women nor any children; only men. Neither were there any horses or other beasts of burden to be seen; the carts were propelled by some force I could not see, but which I guessed to be electricity. All of it was illuminated by what appeared to be hundreds of Edison lamps, hanging from wires or mounted on the buildings.

As I gazed out across this wonderland there came a much louder crackle than the norm, and a sudden flash – an electric discharge, I thought – from the top of one of the domes. Most of the men ignored it, but continued about their various activities. A few glanced up, but then carried on.

No one noticed me – but then, why would anyone bother to look at the top of the wall?

I pulled myself up and swung my feet around until I was sitting atop the wall, my bag beside me. Looking straight down, I made the interesting discovery that the wall was not noticeably thicker at the base than at the top; the entire structure leaned inward, making it easy to climb on the outside, but significantly more difficult on the inside. That would fit if this were some sort of prison, but those lamps and wires and carts and domes certainly did not look like features of any prison with which I was familiar.

A new humming began somewhere amid those mysterious structures, rising in pitch until it became a painful whine, and then dropping again. No one I could see seemed to pay any attention.

Immediately below me, under the overhanging wall, lay what appeared to be a storage yard, where several stacks of wooden beams and copper bars were arranged. None of the buildings in the enclosure were built directly against the wall; a gap of at least five or six feet seemed to separate them all from the surrounding barrier, and these stored structural materials were piled in that gap. If I were to fall from my perch I would only have a drop of perhaps twelve to fifteen feet, but I would land atop one of the stacks. I suspected that such an impact would make quite a racket, as the stacks did not appear to be of particularly tight construction, and the experience might be painful – those were hard materials. I estimated that lowering myself over the side until I hung from my hands would reduce the drop to six or eight feet and make a safe landing more likely, but I still thought it would probably be noisy.

Fortunately, I thought, I had another option; I had ten feet of stout cord in my shoulder bag. I looked about for somewhere I might secure one end to the top of the wall.

There were no obvious anchorages, but I leaned forward and felt under the edge and found that the wall's interior surface was not as seamless as the exterior. The protective layer of tin was secured to a horizontal beam, and by using one of my knives I was able to pry up the edge of the metal sheeting and feel along the seam between this beam and the wall's main structure until I found a small gap – perhaps a knothole originally, but at any rate an opening big enough for me to push one end of the rope through it. I was then able to catch that end back up and tie a slipknot, making a loop around the beam. That gave me perhaps seven or eight feet of cord hanging straight down.

Moving very carefully, as silently as I could, and hoping that no one in the enclosure happened to look up at the wrong moment, I swung myself over the edge and lowered myself down the rope, stretching my toes downward, hoping I would be able to reach the top of one of the tallest of those stacks – specifically, a stack of wooden beams.

I could not *quite* manage it, but I came close enough that I allowed myself to drop the last foot or so, hoping that the stacked wood was as sturdy as it looked.

It was sturdy enough. There was a brief clatter, but it was not particularly loud, and nothing fell. I landed in a crouch, straightened up carefully, and then climbed down the stack to the ground. Fortunately, as I had observed from above, the wooden beams were loosely stacked, providing footholds for my descent.

Throughout the climb I felt dreadfully exposed, as the glow of a thousand electric lights shone from the more inhabited and active areas of the enclosure, through the gaps between buildings into this storage area.

Once on the ground I was quick to wedge my bag into the narrow space between the woodpile and the wall; I did not want to be burdened with those supplies while I was exploring. When that was done I took advantage of the shadows between the stacks and the buildings to conceal myself.

This illicit entry was easy enough that I wondered just how seriously the builders of this place took their own security. I won't say that just *anyone* could have gotten in as I did, but I had managed it with only a very little improvised equipment; any serious invader would have brought ropes and ladders and made short work of it.

But then I realized that the walls were probably not intended to keep anyone *out*; in all likelihood their purpose was to keep people *in*. I guessed that at least some of these men were prisoners.

At any rate, I was inside. I debated, as I crouched in the shadows, just how I might best continue my explorations; should I walk around in the open, as if I belonged here and hope that no one would realize I did not? Or should I instead skulk about, trying to stay out of sight?

Skulking had some inherent problems. If I *were* to be spotted, I might not even realize it immediately; I could be followed, cornered, and trapped. It would be obvious I was up to something I shouldn't be. There were places I would be unable to go at all.

I therefore chose to risk exploring openly, though I intended to always keep a clear path to an exit – either my rope, or a gate, should I see one.

Of course, even from the top of the stack the rope was almost out of reach, and grabbing it to climb out would be something of a challenge, especially if I had pursuers trying to stop me. Still, I thought I could manage it.

I knew that I needed to look as if I belonged; I couldn't just wander aimlessly. I looked down the nearest of the narrow streets – little more than an alley, though as wide as any I had seen, as yet – and picked a building. That, I told myself, was where I was going – not in a desperate hurry, but that was my destination. Then I walked out of the storage yard, neither rushing nor dawdling. I looked around, not as if I was unfamiliar with my surroundings, but as if I was seeing how my neighborhood was doing.

It seemed to be doing pretty well. A few people glanced at me, and some of them looked puzzled, but no one appeared particularly surprised or alarmed by my presence. Perhaps my hatless, coatless, and somewhat disheveled appearance confused them.

The buildings were all of wood, and of the cheapest, shoddiest construction; nowhere was any brick or stone to be seen. There were few windows, and those few were mostly small and high enough to give no view of any interiors. Electrical equipment was on every side, mounted on walls or hanging from wires or sitting in niches and alleyways – blackened wood, copper rods, and glittering crystals were everywhere. Some of this equipment I recognized, but much of it was utterly mysterious. Every so often there was a shower of sparks, or a sharp crackle, or some other manifestation to show that yes, these mysterious devices were operating and were electrical in nature. Some of them were being tended by men in laboratory coats or workmen in overalls, while others were functioning without visible supervision.

An electrical wonderland, I thought – but what was it all for? Who were these men?

I had almost reached my arbitrary destination and was starting to worry about what I should do when I got there, when a voice exclaimed, "Mr. Derringer? Is that you? What are *you* doing here?"

Chapter Nine

I Find the Professor

I turned, expecting to see Mr. de la Rue or someone equally unwelcome, but discovered Professor Vanderhart himself, standing in an open doorway between two mysterious columns of wood and wire, gaping at me. He seemed a little thinner than I remembered him, but was still a very large man – only of medium height, but quite stout.

No, let me be honest; "stout" does not do him justice. He was fat. His blond hair was still uncombed, as it had always been when I saw him in the past, but he wore a new coat and no hat. I envied him that coat, as even inside the walls and out of the wind the weather was quite chilly, especially as my clothing was not yet entirely dry.

"Ah, Professor!" I said. "Could you spare a moment, perhaps?"

"I suppose I could – but really, why are you...?"

I held up a hand. "Could we go inside?"

"Well, I was on my way...but yes, yes, that can wait. Come in, come in!" He stood aside and gestured for me to enter.

I squeezed past and found myself in a windowless room that was in fact of moderate dimensions, but which felt small and crowded because much of it was full of pipes and glass tubes of various shapes and sizes, running up, down, across, and in coils along every wall and much of the ceiling, all of it illuminated with Edison lamps. A table covered with papers occupied the center of the room, and a single large wooden chair stood beside it. Books were stacked on the floor to either side, and a small, overstuffed bookcase occupied the only patch of wall not covered by plumbing.

Professor Vanderhart looked at that chair, then at me, and said, "Come in here," as he led the way to a door on the far side that I had hardly noticed amidst the glassware and plumbing. That opened into a comfortable little bed–sitting room where a cozy fire was burning on a brick hearth, keeping out the unseasonable chill of that April evening. An unlit oil lamp stood on a small bedside table, the first I had seen in this place. There was a desk, its top rolled down, and an accompanying office chair, but there were also two red velvet chairs in the style of the Second French Empire on either side of a gilt tea table.

The professor directed me to one of the velvet chairs, while he took the other; it creaked under his weight. He glanced at the bedside lamp but left it as it was, instead relying on the gentle orange glow of the fire, and the yellow glare through the open door, to illuminate the room.

"Now, Mr. Derringer," he said. "What are you doing in this outpost of Monsieur Boireau's empire?"

"Why, looking for *you*, Professor! Your family is very concerned."

"My family? Concerned?" He frowned. "Is there a problem? Are they well?"

"They were all well as of a few days ago, yes, but they are tremendously worried not to have heard from you."

"Haven't heard?" He stared at me, eyes wide. "Haven't they been getting my letters?"

"Letters?" I shook my head. "Your wife has received no letters."

At that he looked thunderstruck. "I have been writing to her three times a week, every week, on Monday, Wednesday, and Friday, without fail!" he exclaimed. "I posted them all..." He let that sentence trail off, then continued, "Well, no. I gave them to

Monsieur Boireau's messengers to post for me. Are you telling me that *none* of them were delivered?"

"Not a one, sir, and Mrs. Vanderhart has been worried half to death. She wired Betsy and me to come find you as soon as I could, so we rushed back from the Utah Territory to lend whatever aid we could. Betsy is at home, caring for her mother, and I have come looking for you."

"But that's ridiculous! Why would she be worried? Didn't anyone tell her what I was doing?"

I suppressed an urge to shout and kept my voice to a normal, if emphatic, tone. "*No,* sir, they did not," I said. "The last report anyone had of you was when you were forcibly abducted by Leopold de la Rue outside the New Brunswick railroad station."

"I wasn't... well, yes, I *was* abducted, I suppose, but it was...well, not actually a misunderstanding so much as an expedient." He waved his hands, though I was not quite sure what this gesture was intended to convey. "They felt that it was urgent I join Boireau's project immediately and not dither about deciding whether or not to take the job."

"Job?"

"*Yes,* Mr. Derringer, the job!" He sounded exasperated. "I am working for Monsieur Boireau, researching ways to cope with high pressures, among other things, and a requirement of my employment is that I stay here, in this compound, at all times. Didn't anyone *tell* Mary?"

"*No,*" I said emphatically. "No one received any word of your whereabouts whatsoever."

At that, he appeared not so much exasperated as distraught. "That de la Rue *promised* someone would go by the house that very evening and tell her I was delayed!"

"I regret to say, sir, that no one did."

"But that's...that's absolutely heartless!"

"I cannot disagree."

"You implied that my wife was in a state of near collapse,

and Betsy had come home to attend to her – is that the case?"

"It is."

"And the other children?"

"I did not speak to them, but they appeared well enough. Upset by your absence, of course, but well enough."

He was regaining his calm. "Well, at least *that's* something. I shall have to write an apology and send it with you."

"Yes, sir." I hesitated, then said, "This job you have taken requires you to stay here and have no contact with the outside world?"

"Stay here, yes, but I had *thought* I was in contact with my family and friends. There is no telegraph office nor telephone service here on Wildwood Island, but we were *told* that the mail service operated normally. I was rather dismayed that Mary had not replied, but I had assumed it was merely pique at the abruptness of my departure."

"I am afraid it was far more than pique."

"But if my letters weren't received, then how did you *find* me?"

I explained the entire sequence of events. "...and I consider it quite an extraordinary bit of luck that you happened to recognize me and call my name," I concluded.

"Well, I was on my way to get my supper," he replied. "This enclave is not really very large, after all; if we were both roaming the streets it wasn't unlikely we would meet."

"I suppose," I said. "But now, Professor, you've heard my story; would you please return the favor and tell me what you're doing here and how it came to happen?"

The professor frowned. "I'm not supposed to talk to anyone about it. Well, no one except my fellow scientists."

"Is that why this job requires you to stay here? To maintain secrecy?"

"It is. We have all been asked to remain here at all times, and we have been paid well for the inconvenience. I'll be honest,

Mr. Derringer, while my job here is interesting, and because I was already on sabbatical it did not interfere with my position at the college, my primary reason for accepting it was that Monsieur Boireau is paying *very* generously – every Wednesday morning, in cash, without fail. And he fears that anyone who leaves the compound might let something slip, so remaining here is a requirement of our employment. He's quite convinced his enemies have spies everywhere."

"He has enemies?"

"He thinks so."

"Do *you* think so?"

"I am not in a position to say."

"Professor, do you think *I* am one of his enemies?"

"It does seem very unlikely."

"Then could you *please* tell me what is going on here? I give you my word I will keep it in confidence."

"Oh, well," he said, "do you know the nature of Monsieur Boireau's project?"

"No," I said. "I understand it has some connection with the Lost City of the Mirage, but beyond that, no. Nor do I know who this Sebastien Boireau *is*."

"He's a French millionaire. His great grandfather won some fantastic monetary award from the Emperor Napoleon – the first one, not that more recent fool – for a secret discovery, the nature of which I do not know, and that served as the foundation of the family's fortunes. His family has built well upon that foundation, and he is immensely wealthy. Beyond that, I have not troubled myself with details."

"I see," I said. "And what is this project of his?"

Professor Vanderhart grimaced, and considered for a moment before saying, "I suppose that as an adventurer, you know something about the Lost City of the Mirage?"

"I have never seen it, but I know a fair amount of its history, yes," I agreed.

"Well, Monsieur Boireau got interested in it because he learned that the City contains mysterious devices that are apparently electrical in nature. Electricity is a part of his family's heritage – that secret discovery his ancestor made had something to do with electricity – so he began studying the place, though he hasn't yet managed to visit it, and he learned that not only is it reported to be absolutely *littered* with what appear to be electrical devices, none of which function, but that the City is becoming less ruinous over time – which is, of course, quite contrary to the natural way of things."

"What?" I said, startled. I am not proud of this vague question, but I was taken quite off my guard.

"The City is becoming less ruinous with each appearance," the professor explained. "If a wall is reported to have crumbled at the time of one visit, by the next that very same wall may well be intact. In the earliest reports that are even remotely reliable, the City was little more than scattered heaps of stone, rather like many ordinary ruins; in its more recent appearances there are recognizable streets, many of them paved, lined with partial – or by some reports, even complete – buildings. Lampposts have appeared; I know you have heard about the many aluminum posts and railings that Hezekiah McKee hauled out of the City at its most recent appearance, but earlier reports say that no such posts or railings existed in previous manifestations."

I had, in fact, heard vague accounts along these lines, but had not taken them very seriously. If I thought about it at all, I had assumed that wind was uncovering more of the City each time it appeared. Walls being rebuilt, though, were not so easily explained.

"Go on," I said.

"Well, our friend Monsieur Boireau found this very concerning. He concluded that while the City was being looted every time it appeared in *our* world, the rest of the time it must exist *somewhere else*, and that while it was in this other realm someone was adding to it, gradually restoring and rebuilding it."

"That's an interesting theory," I said, though I immediately detected certain problems with it.

"Isn't it? At any rate, Boireau believes that these mysterious builders are adding to the Lost City because they intend, once it has been suitably prepared, to ride it into *our* world as the first step in an invasion, using their incredibly advanced electrical weapons to overwhelm any resistance."

"I...don't see that as the only explanation," I said. In truth, I thought it a very *unlikely* explanation; I could see several serious flaws in it.

"Well, I don't know that I would, either, but Monsieur Boireau does. After years of study, he claims to have accumulated all the evidence he needs to prove it, and to disprove every other explanation that has been suggested."

"All right," I said. "For the sake of argument, I will accept that. And where does this leave us?"

The professor sighed. "Boireau says that he approached the French government with his theory and was dismissed; those who did not think him mad said that a single City little more than a mile across could not pose much of a threat to any modern nation, and they would leave it to adventurers visiting the Lost City to keep them informed of any dangers – and most likely to eliminate those dangers without spending any tax money on it."

"I might have said the same," I admitted.

"Other governments, if they agreed to hear him at all, were no more cooperative than the Third Republic. After all, he's a Frenchman. So he resolved to take care of it himself. He has built himself his own little empire, with hidden enclaves like this one scattered around the world. He has gathered together all the experts on electricity he could find who were willing to work for him – Edison turned him down, unfortunately, and is too well known a public figure to be taken against his will. He is hoping these scientists and inventors will be able to figure out some of the devices captured from the City, or that they may find ways to make formidable electrical weapons of our own."

"*That's* what this place is for?" I exclaimed. "That's why those scientists vanished? He brought them here to develop electrical weapons?"

"Exactly – well, here, or his other outposts."

"Wait – what about the missing adventurers?"

"He wants them to serve as his scouts when the Lost City next appears, as well as running various errands for him in the meantime."

"And what does he want with *you*?" I asked. "I mean no offense, Professor Vanderhart, but electricity is not your field."

"No, but – well, he has *another* theory."

"Oh?"

"Yes, he's been trying to chart the Lost City's appearances, so he can predict where and when the next might occur..."

"Several people have attempted that," I interrupted.

"Oh, I know, and so does he," the professor said with a dismissive wave. "But he thinks he may have a new angle to consider. I'm sure you know, Mr. Derringer, that much of the Earth's surface is covered with water – the oceans make up more than twice as much area as the continents."

"Yes."

"Well, it's one of Monsieur Boireau's theories that one reason we've had such difficulty in finding a pattern in the Lost City's manifestations is that many of them happen underwater. We are missing several key data points, and it may be that those are at the bottom of the ocean."

I had to admit that there was a certain logic to that.

"He had another idea, as well – that the great explosion in the East Indies might have had some connection with the Lost City."

"The explosion you went to study?"

The professor nodded. "I took a sabbatical year from my position at Rutgers so that I could visit the site, an island called Krakatoa – though most of the island is now gone, destroyed by the blast. While that was fascinating in itself, I saw no indication at all that it might be connected to the Lost City. It was simply an ordinary volcano, albeit one far more powerful and destructive than the norm. The explosion was quite spectacular, but there was nothing mysterious about it."

"But Monsieur Boireau sent his assistant, Leopold de la Rue, to interview you about it?"

"Yes, exactly. And although nothing about my visit to Krakatoa seemed in any way relevant, Mr. de la Rue found other areas where he thought my expertise might be valuable. As professor of natural history in Rutgers Scientific School much of my work is in mechanics, and I take a particular interest in the effects of high and low pressure – the airship I sold you was one result of that. And he was interested in what I told him about your adventures with Reverend McKee and the aluminum he took from the Lost City."

That, I guessed, was why Monsieur Boireau had been so determined to interview me.

"He brought me here to determine what effects there might be if the City had manifested at various depths beneath the ocean, and where in the ocean it might or might not have appeared." He gestured toward the outer room and its bizarre contents. "That's what I've been working on these last few weeks."

"And have you made any significant findings?"

"Not really, no. I simply don't have enough information about the Lost City. No one has ever tested the City's structures for how much pressure they can survive, and that is not something that can be done from a distance. No one has searched the foundations for lingering seawater. I have submitted what results I could for Boireau's consideration, but I doubt they would be of any use."

"Then is there any reason to stay here? Your wife is *very* concerned."

"Perhaps not," the professor agreed. He glanced warily at the door. "But I am not certain I will be *allowed* to leave."

Chapter Ten

Professor Vanderhart Imprisoned

"Do you think you are a *prisoner* here?" I asked.

"I don't know," he admitted. "I think I might be. I did not think so until today, but now that you tell me no one knows where I am, or even that I am still alive – if Monsieur Boireau is so devoted to secrecy as all that, it seems unlikely he will allow me to leave."

I had suspected as much. "You think this is all for the sake of secrecy? That rather than hiring you and your fellows to work in an ordinary laboratory, he had this entire place built to so that he might keep your work hidden from the rest of the world?"

"I would assume so. From the terms of my employment I would say that Monsieur Boireau is unquestionably trying to keep his projects here a secret."

"From *whom*?" I asked.

The professor hesitated, as if gathering his wits, then said, "He seems to think that whatever group is rebuilding the Lost City has an extensive network of spies in their employ, and that any conversation outside these walls might be overheard by one of them. He says that no one is to be trusted, not even our friends and family; the enemy has agents everywhere. Even in those letters you say were never delivered, I was instructed to say nothing of my whereabouts or the nature of my research."

I thought this sounded completely ridiculous, but I said merely, "That does not seem very reasonable to me."

"That the agents of this mysterious power behind the Lost

City are everywhere, spying on everyone? I cannot say I find it very likely, myself – but it's Boireau's opinion that matters, and he appears absolutely convinced of it."

"And you think he will keep you in here by force, to maintain this secrecy?"

"He might." He sighed. "I am not being held in any obvious way," he continued. "I am treated as if I were a free man. I receive my pay every Wednesday, and I have now tucked away a tidy sum. I am provided with this apartment and my meals, and since I was taken away without a chance to pack, I have been supplied with the necessities of life – clothing, soap, razor, hairbrush, and so on. I can move freely about the compound, and speak to whomever I please. But am I free to leave? I don't know."

"Perhaps you should test it," I suggested. "Just walk to the gate and ask to go."

"Perhaps I should," he replied, but I could tell from his expression that he was not yet prepared to do so.

Rather than press the issue immediately, I remarked, "I see at least one significant problem with Monsieur Boireau's theories."

"Oh?"

"The Lost City has been appearing and disappearing for *centuries*. How can this scheme to use it as the vanguard of an invasion make any sense, in light of that?"

"No one ever said that these invaders are *human*, Mr. Derringer. Presumably they live far longer than we do."

"And yet they employ a vast network of human agents to spy for them?"

"So Monsieur Boireau professes to believe."

"Well, to pursue such an endeavor for so long would certainly require inhuman *patience*," I acknowledged. "And they do not seem to be in any hurry. Empires have arisen and fallen, and entire cities have been built from raw wilderness, in the time it has taken these creatures to transform a crumbling ruin into a somewhat less-crumbled one."

"I..." He frowned. "When you put it that way, it does sound unlikely. But perhaps they only have access to the City for brief periods, as *we* do."

"I still find the proposed schedule hard to accept," I said. "What's more, for them to have gone completely undetected by the Lost City's visitors until now, they would need to have known when it would appear and disappear, so that they might deliver their workers as soon as the City became accessible, and remove them without the slightest trace before it returned to our plane of existence."

"Perhaps they are *controlling* when it appears and disappears."

"Then why do they allow it to appear in our world to be explored and looted every so often, instead of keeping it out of sight until they are ready to launch their invasion? It makes no sense."

The professor shrugged. "Well, you are welcome to argue it with Monsieur Boireau. *I* am only concerned with whether the City has spent time deep below the sea."

"And has it?"

"As I rather thought I had said, I can't tell. We simply don't have the evidence to make that determination."

"But it *could* have?"

"I don't see why not."

"Have the electrical devices your fellow scientists are working with been corroded by seawater?"

He hesitated. "It's hard to be sure," he said. "Many of the samples were sealed inside cases of metal or glass or...or other substances. There are materials in the Lost City no one has as yet identified; metallic aluminum is only *one* of the mysterious substances found there, and one of the less-mysterious ones, at that. And the devices are so *strange* – if anything gives support to Monsieur Boireau's belief in non–human builders, it is the utterly alien nature of those fragments."

"Fragments?"

"Well, since none of them seem to *do* anything, and most are quite small, we assume they are merely fragments of much larger machines."

I nodded. "Weapons, do you think?"

"Actually, no. I do not think they are weapons. But I have no idea what they *are*. Or rather, what they *were*, since none of them seem to operate. Most of them are incredibly intricate."

"You know, I have read and heard a fair bit about the Lost City," I said, "and I have not encountered much about these things."

"Well, until fairly recently, no one had realized they were *machines*, rather than mere ornaments," the professor said. "Their electrical nature was only recognized in the last five years or so, and is still the subject of some debate. There are some who suggest they operated on some principle as yet unknown to science, perhaps using some other form of energy entirely, akin to Sir Edward Bulwer–Lytton's 'vril.' But Monsieur Boireau, and the scientists he has gathered here, believe them to be electrical, largely because many of them are connected to what appear to be batteries – though the chemistry of those batteries is unlike anything with which we are familiar."

"And these devices are what cause the occasional electrical displays I have seen here?"

"What, *here*? Oh, good heavens, no! No, those buzzes and flashes are all made by the inventions of my fellow employees. No, the most anyone has coaxed from any of the Lost City devices without destroying them is a faint glow."

"Then why does Monsieur Boireau see them as such a threat?"

"You would have to ask *him*; I cannot say."

"I may do that." In fact, I was becoming ever more convinced that I needed to have another conversation with M. Boireau.

At that, there was a brief lull in our conversation that ended when Professor Vanderhart got to his feet.

"While this has been a very interesting discussion, Mr. Derringer, and I do hope you will let my family know that I am alive and well, right now I am late for my supper, and frankly, I'm hungry. Would you care to join me?"

I had not eaten since luncheon, and the idea of food was anything but repulsive, but I hesitated. "Will no one notice a stranger at supper?"

"Oh, I don't think so. You were not stopped before, were you? You walked openly down the street. None of us know everyone here, and other men arrive every so often from Monsieur Boireau's other outposts."

I arose. "You must tell me more about this empire of his," I said. "You can do so while we eat, perhaps?"

"I should be delighted."

And with that, we quitted his rooms and emerged once again onto the street, where he led the way to the dining pavilion. Once there and seated, a young man took our order – there were only limited choices, rather than a full menu, and I let the professor choose for me. We had only a brief wait before plates of roast beef and boiled potatoes were set before us, accompanied by generous mugs of beer.

The pavilion held perhaps a dozen tables of varying sizes; we had taken one of the smallest, in a relatively quiet corner. No one at the other tables paid any attention to us; any concerns I had had of drawing unwanted notice proved groundless.

The pavilion itself was very plain, whitewashed wood walls, ceilings, and posts, and varnished pine floors; its most remarkable feature was that like so much of the compound, it was lit with strings of Edison lamps.

While we waited for our food, and again while we ate, the professor explained the compound's arrangements. This was home for the scientists and their laboratories, who lived within the sloping walls, while the staff – cooks, cleaners, laboratory assistants, guards, and so on – lived with their families in the cabins I had seen to the south, and came to the enclosure to work, serving twelve-hour shifts.   Only men were permitted inside the compound, but of course the village's population included women and children. I had been fortunate that I had not arrived during a shift change, when the road past the enclosure's east side would have been lined with workers coming and going.

M. Boireau claimed to have sixteen such enclaves scattered around the world, with two in the United States, the other being on an island in the Washington Territory. Most of the rest were in Europe, with others in Australia, Africa, China, and Brazil. He had recruited, voluntarily or otherwise, *hundreds* of scientists and mechanicians. He had invested a large part of his family fortune in this, purportedly out of an altruistic determination to save all mankind from the threat he saw posed by the Lost City of the Mirage.

I questioned whether he was actually as pure of heart as that, and Professor Vanderhart agreed that he almost certainly hoped to profit from some of the devices his employees would create.

At any rate, every so often men from one of the other enclaves would arrive to compare notes with their American counterparts, and every so often one of the Americans would disappear, reportedly sent to another location.

A thought struck me, and I asked whether any of Boireau's researchers were female; I knew that there were many women capable of scientific brilliance, and the professor's own daughter was a superb mechanician.

"No," he told me, as he cut himself a bite of beef. "I had asked about that myself, and Monsieur Boireau dismissed the notion as absurd. He believes that allowing any women in his little enclosures would serve as too great a distraction. Even our cooks and housekeepers here are all male. The women of the village tend to their own homes, but are kept away from us." He shrugged. "I think he's making a mistake, that having women around would improve the atmosphere even if he cannot find any he thinks worthy as researchers, but it's his money he's spending, so he can do as he pleases."

I thought it a shame that so much talent might be going to waste simply because it was in the minds and hearts and hands of the fairer sex, and I wondered whether there might be some way to employ all that untapped ability – but I am merely an adventurer, not in a position to attempt such an enterprise.

The scientists, I was informed, whether domestic or foreign, remained always inside the compound, free from any distractions – not just the presence of women and children, but also any news from the outside world, anything that might give them something to think about other than their research. I thought this, too, was a mistake – after all, many great insights had come about through serendipity, such as the apple that had supposedly fallen upon Sir Isaac Newton and inspired his theory of gravitation. Some chance tidbit in the daily news might result in a great discovery. Again, though, it was Monsieur Boireau's choice.

The other workers were checked in and out at the gate, but the scientists – well, Professor Vanderhart said *he* had never seen any of them leave the compound. Each man had a small apartment like the professor's and ate at the dining pavilion.

Every Wednesday afternoon a carefully guarded payroll chest would arrive, and wages would be distributed to every employee, both the scientists and the service staff. I remarked on this – since there was nowhere for anyone to *spend* that money in the compound, what became of the money paid to the scientists?

"I can't speak for anyone else," the professor replied, "but I keep mine securely hidden away. I have a goodly sum accumulated already."

"If everyone does that," I said, "then it seems to me that this place would be quite a fine target for thieves."

"I suppose it would, if they knew it was here."

I did not pursue the matter, but in the back of my mind I could not help considering the possibilities inherent in the situation. The line between thieves and adventurers was not very sharply drawn, to put it politely, and Monsieur Boireau had recruited a few dozen adventurers, as well as his hundreds of scientists. They surely had some idea of the situation. Had any of them given any thought to going after all that accumulated treasure? Having it scattered among hundreds of recipients in sixteen different places around the world would make the task somewhat more challenging, of course, but that was hardly an insurmountable obstacle for someone accustomed to battling monsters and robbing ancient tombs.

I did not say a word of that aloud, of course.

"So Monsieur Boireau is the ruler of this electrical empire," I said, "which is entirely devoted to developing defenses against an anticipated attack from the Lost City of the Mirage. What happens if no attack comes?"

"I have no idea," the professor said. "You would have to ask Monsieur Boireau."

When we had eaten, and the waiter had cleared away our plates, we arose and strolled back toward the professor's rooms. Artificial lightning arced overhead more than once, sparks showered from various devices and overhead wires, and I thought I saw a look of recognition on the face of someone we passed in the street, but he did not say anything.

If he had in truth recognized me, though, what of it? He would assume I was simply one more adventurer in Monsieur Boireau's employ – as in fact, I might well have been, had I stayed in New York. Besides, he might well have just been wondering what I was doing out in such raw weather with no hat or coat.

At the door of his residence, the professor hesitated. "Would you like to come in?"

I shook my head. "No, Professor, I think I have learned most of what I came to learn. There are one or two points that remain, but I don't believe we can find those answers in your rooms."

"Oh?"

"First, are you indeed a prisoner? Perhaps you could talk to the guards at the gate and determine that."

"I don't..." he began.

"You would not ask them straight out, of course," I interrupted. "Instead, inquire as to when the next boat leaves tomorrow and whether you could take it to the mainland."

"Oh." He frowned. "I suppose I could do *that*. And your second point?"

"If you *are* being held here, would you like me to help you escape?"

Chapter Eleven

My Escape from the Empire

I stayed well back, my hands in my pockets, trying to look as if my presence were merely a coincidence, while Professor Vanderhart approached the man seated by the gate.

The gate was a fairly simple thing – a heavy wooden door, broad and tall enough to admit a large wagon, painted the same gray as the walls, and held shut by an iron bolt the size of a man's forearm. The bolt was secured in place with a massive black padlock passed through a hole behind a bracket. A single guard sat at a table to one side, reading a newspaper; since the professor had told me newspapers were not allowed in the compound, I wondered about that. Perhaps an exception was made for the guards, or perhaps this man had smuggled his in.

"Excuse me," Professor Vanderhart said, a trifle more loudly than would seem entirely natural. I supposed this was for my benefit, but the impression was rather that he was himself hard of hearing.

The guard looked up, but did not put down his paper. "Yes?"

"I was wondering, my good man – when does the first boat leave tomorrow? I should very much like to visit the mainland."

At that, the guard folded the paper and set it aside. He pulled over a notebook that I had not noticed before; the newspaper had concealed it.

It had also concealed a revolver.

"Your name, sir?" he asked, as he opened the notebook.

"Aloysius Vanderhart," the professor replied.

"Vanderhart? You're one of the scientists, sir?" He glanced at the notebook and turned a page, then looked up again. "From the Rutgers Scientific School?"

"Why, yes."

"Then I'm sorry, sir, but you are not to leave the island. In fact, unless you can provide some documentation that you need to collect samples elsewhere on the island, I'm afraid I have instructions not to allow you to leave the experimental enclave at all."

"What? But I'm a free man!"

"I'm following my orders, sir. Mr. de la Rue was very clear, and if there were any doubt, I have my written instructions right here." He tapped the notebook. "I can have a letter mailed, if you like."

"No, thank you. I must say, though, I am very disappointed in our employers! I shall have to have a word with Mr. de la Rue."

"You're welcome to do that, sir. He will be here with the payroll on Wednesday, as always."

The professor pursed his lips, and rose up on the balls of his feet, then settled back on his heels. I wondered whether he might have more to say, or might try to push past and open the gate himself, but he did not; he just stood and glowered. The guard had nothing more to say, but simply waited, one hand on the notebook and the other on his newspaper, until at last the professor turned and strode away.

I joined him perhaps a hundred feet down the street.

"I'm afraid I'm not surprised," I said.

"Neither am I," he admitted. "I had hoped we might have misjudged the situation, but it seems we did not."

"I think our next step is to see whether we can leave by some other route."

"Yes. How did you get *in* here, Mr. Derringer?"

"I'll be happy to show you, Professor."

And with that, I led him to the storage yard and pointed out my rope. "I climbed in on that," I said. I hesitated, trying to think of a polite way to phrase what I had to say. "I expect to leave the same way," I said, "but I am not sure whether a man of your age and condition would be able to do the same."

He looked up at the rope in silence for a moment, then said, "And if I somehow did clamber up that rope – which I don't think I can, so this is purely hypothetical – then what? We're on an island; do you have a boat hidden away somewhere?"

"Alas, I do not," I said. "You have been too polite to comment on my lack of civilized outer garments, sir, but I'm sure you noticed I have no coat or hat; this is because I *swam* to the island from a hired boat. I have arranged a rendezvous for it to retrieve me from the far end of the island in the morning, but it will, of necessity, stand offshore some distance, to avoid running aground. We would need to swim out to it."

"I can't swim. Or at least, not well. How far would I need to go?"

"I can't say for sure. Perhaps fifty or a hundred yards?"

He shuddered and shook his head. "That's not possible. Not for me. And you said the far end of the island – you plan to walk there in the dark?"

"I do."

He shook his head. "I do not think I am up to such an adventure."

I could scarcely argue. "I feared as much. In that case, sir, you will not be leaving this compound tonight. However, *I* will be, and I will take word of your situation to Mrs. Vanderhart. I will also discuss it with local law enforcement; I do not believe Monsieur Boireau has any right to hold you captive here. That would constitute kidnapping and false imprisonment."

"I'm not sure what local law enforcement there *is* here."

"Neither am I, but I intend to find out."

He nodded.

"One way or another, Professor, I will be back," I promised. With that, I retrieved my bag, hoisted it to my shoulder, and began climbing the stack of lumber. When I had reached the top of the pile I looked down.

Professor Vanderhart waved farewell, and turned away.

I watched him go, then focused my attention on the dangling end of my rope, hanging perhaps two feet above my head – or perhaps a little more. I jumped, grabbed – and missed, and was very glad no one was watching, as my foot slipped and I took an awkward tumble on the pile of lumber, only just managing to not fall off the side. I paused for a moment, making sure no one had heard the clatter and come looking for the cause; given the constant noises from the electrical equipment I did not think it likely, but preferred to err on the side of caution.

When no one came I got carefully to my feet for another try. I waited until the rope, which I had batted in my previous attempt even if I had not caught it, stopped moving significantly, then took another leap.

This time I caught the rope and managed to hang on, though I lost a little skin from the palm of my hand before I was able to get a solid grip. I twisted the cord around one forearm and pulled myself up, stretching out with my feet until they bumped against the wall.

Next time, I promised myself, I would bring a longer rope, or find a different route in. Perhaps I could go *through* the wall, instead of over it – after all, it was just wood. An axe might work. That probably could not go undetected, though.

I began hauling myself up. It grew easier as I rose, as my feet were able to find better purchase on the wall, and it was not long before I was able to swing myself up onto the top.

There I paused to catch my breath and looked back down into the enclave.

The various electrical experiments certainly generated plenty of light and sound and frequent showers of sparks, but I had no idea whether any of them could be useful as weapons. Perhaps I should have stayed longer and spoken with Professor Vanderhart at greater length about what his colleagues were up to, but I was not about to turn back now. Instead I hauled the rope up, swung it over to the outside of the enclosure, and made my way back down to the sand and scrub.

It was much, much darker outside than it had been on the electrically lit streets. Full night had fallen, and if the moon was up – I did not remember where in its cycle it might be – it was completely hidden by the heavy overcast. I could hear the surf, I could feel the cold wind, and I could see the glow above the wooden walls, but other than that I could make out almost nothing of my surroundings.

That was the moment when the rain that had been threatening all evening began to fall in earnest. I sighed, and began walking southward, stumbling every so often over a rock, a shrub, or a chunk of driftwood.

I was soaked to the skin and shivering with cold in minutes.

In time my eyes did adjust, and I continued cautiously to the south with fewer mishaps. I gave the workers' village a wide berth; fortunately, the rain kept its residents inside, though I could hear faint snatches of conversation and childish laughter. Apparently the workers were allowed to have their families present, even if the scientists were not.

It took at least an hour, probably considerably more, to reach the tip of the island, but at last I came to a point where I stood on a triangle of sand with water to both east and west, as well as straight ahead.

I assumed I was overlooking the Cape May Inlet, but I saw only water. I stood on the sand, staring out into the rain, trying to catch a glimpse of the land on the far side. I could not. I could not even be sure there *was* any land directly across from where I stood; it was entirely possible that Wildwood Island extended farther east than the point on the other side of the channel. Albert had said the narrowest part of the inlet was only three hundred yards across, but I had no way of knowing, in the dark, where the narrowest part *was*. I had thought I might glimpse the lights of the town in the distance, but I did not.

I had not, until this moment, completely abandoned the idea of swimming back to Cape May, but staring into the night I decided that I would wait and see whether Albert did return in the morning, as he had promised.

I hoped the rain would not deter him, should it continue through the night.

I sat down, set my bag beside me, then huddled as best I could with no hat or coat, and sat, shivering, waiting for dawn.

Of course, I fell asleep. I started awake to find the sun clearing the horizon. I was cold, stiff, and utterly drenched, but the rain had lessened to the merest drizzle, and the clouds had lifted enough to allow the golden light of morning to reach me.

I got to my feet, stretched, and looked around. I saw no sign of anyone but myself. Even my footprints had been largely erased by the rain.

Taking my directions from the sun I looked to the south, beyond the end of the island. I saw only open ocean. I shuddered, glad I had not attempted to swim to Cape May. Turning to the west I could see land in the distance, but even in ideal conditions that would have been a challenging crossing, and in the cold waters of that chilly April I doubted I would survive it.

I could not bring myself to simply wait and do nothing, though, so after another scan of the horizon to the east and south I picked up my bag and began ambling along the southwestern shore. In truth, I hoped that movement would help me warm myself as much as I was trying to get anywhere.

Albert had said he would come looking for me "first thing in the morning," but I had no very clear idea on just what that would mean. For some working people I knew "first thing in the morning" could mean before dawn, while for the idle rich it might just as well mean nine or ten o'clock. Albert was obviously neither idle nor rich, but since his business presumably relied on tourists, he might have adjusted to their schedule.

But no, I had gone scarcely a hundred yards when I saw a sailboat coming up the inlet toward me; perhaps, I mused, Albert kept fisherman's hours in the off season. I stopped and watched, and when I was reasonably sure the approaching vessel was the *Eliza Anne* I began waving my free arm enthusiastically.

After a few moments I saw Albert waving back, and turning his craft toward the shore.

He stopped distressingly far out, however. He cupped his hands around his mouth and called, "This is as close as I can safely bring her!"

I sighed, and sat down to remove my shoes.

The water was even colder than I remembered. Whether the rain had chilled it, or whether the inlet's currents were colder than the waters of the Post Creek basin, or whether my memory was playing tricks on me I cannot say, but when I waded out into the surf I immediately began to tremble.

Still, I had no alternative. I kept going, and when the bottom began to drop away – which was sooner than I had expected – I slung my bag on my shoulder and swam the last twenty yards.

Albert helped me climb out of the water and into the welcoming interior of the *Eliza Anne*, where I collapsed onto a bench, shivering with cold.

"Straight back to the harbor, Mr. Derringer?"

"Yes, please," I managed to say through chattering teeth.

Once we reached the dock I paid Albert for his troubles, thanked him profusely, then walked up through town to the Chalfonte. I had hoped the walk would give my clothes time to dry at least a little, but the lingering drizzle turned back to rain, which put paid to *that* notion. Albert had kept my hat and coat aboard the *Eliza Anne*, so at least I had that additional protection.

At least the rain probably washed away most of the salt; either way, though, I was still badly chilled and eager to get to my room. I hurried past the desk clerk without a word – in fact, I was shivering enough that I was not at all sure I *could* speak. I peeled off my wet garments and tumbled onto the bed, planning to rest for a moment before beginning the day's business.

Naturally, despite my miserable slumber on the beach, I fell asleep again.

When I awoke the morning was well advanced, as I could see in an instant from the sunlight slanting in my window, but the clothes I had so hastily stripped off and dropped in a heap on the floor were still wet; I draped them over a radiator and one side of the bathtub to facilitate further drying. Every time my bare foot hit the wet patch of carpet where they had lain I regretted not attending to them when first I arrived.

I next went through my bag, sorting out its contents and then turning it inside-out to dry.

That done, I dressed and went down to the lobby.

"Good morning, Mr. Derringer!" the desk man said, as I approached.

"Thank you," I said. "I would like to send a telegram, if I may."

He found the pad and prepared to take down my words.

I set out to reassure Betsy and her mother. I wished I had risen earlier, so as not to keep them waiting. The desk clerk assured me he would get my message to Western Union and have it on its way within the hour.

It was a simple message: PROFESSOR ALIVE AND WELL BUT UNABLE TO RETURN HOME IMMEDIATELY STOP. WILL EXPLAIN WHEN I SEE YOU STOP.

And then it was a matter of getting myself a late breakfast and thinking of what my next step should be.

Since the professor and the other scientists were being held against their will, and several of them were the subjects of a widespread search, the obvious thing to do would be to talk to the local officers of the law, but a quick discussion with the waiter revealed that I need not use the plural; there was only one local officer of the law, Mr. William H. Benezet, the sheriff of Cape May County. He had only recently assumed the office and had not yet recruited any deputies, so far as my waiter was aware. The hotels had their own detectives guarding the guests' valuables and making sure order was maintained in their various establishments, but they had no authority off their employers' properties.

I hesitated, unsure whether I should immediately make contact with Mr. Benezet, or whether I should pursue other options. If I called in the law it seemed all too likely that matters would turn violent, and even if our local sheriff had hired a handful of deputies of whom my waiter informant was unaware, the forces of law and order might well be seriously outmanned and outgunned.

There was no great urgency; the scientists were not being mistreated in any way, and it might well be that some of them did not *want* to leave the compound, even once they knew they were prisoners. They were being adequately housed and fed and generously paid.

And if it came to a shoot-out, I had no idea just how dangerous all that electrical equipment might be. Monsieur Boireau was trying to create weapons, after all, and that entire enclosure was built of wood – it would probably burn easily.

It would, I thought, be wise to explore other alternatives before calling on the sheriff. I would visit with Betsy and her mother in New Brunswick to reassure them that Professor Vanderhart was in no immediate danger, and then perhaps go on to New York to discuss matters with Mad Bill Snedeker, with Tobias Arbuthnot, with Dr. Pierce, and with members of the Order of Theseus.

That settled to my own satisfaction, I returned to my room to pack.

Chapter Twelve

The Family Informed

I had gotten a later start than intended after wrapping up my business in Cape May, and as a result I missed my connection on the way to New Brunswick. The next train would have gotten me in too late to reasonably call on the Vanderharts, so I spent the night in Camden before proceeding. The next morning I breakfasted in Camden, but then went directly from my hotel to the station and caught the next northbound train. With my leather bag in one hand and a newly acquired umbrella in the other I walked from the station to my destination, despite the intermittent rain. I could have secured a hack, but I did not mind the exercise after being cooped up on the train, and I was trying to be less profligate with my family's money.

I rang the bell, and after only a very brief interval the front door of the Vanderhart home opened. I was startled to see that Betsy's brother Johannes had answered, rather than an adult; Joe, as he was called, was the elder of the two boys, but still no older than fourteen.

"Yes?" he asked. Then he recognized me. "Oh, Mr. Derringer! Mother's been waiting for you. Please come in!"

I folded my umbrella and obeyed, setting bag and umbrella by the coat rack inside the front door. Rather than presume a welcome that had not yet been given, I kept my hat on. A moment later I found myself in the parlor, where Mrs. Vanderhart, who had been in one of the armchairs, leapt to her feet and demanded, "Where is he? Why can't he come home?"

Betsy had been seated beside her mother; now she rose as

well, and put a restraining hand on her mother's arm. "Mother, please," she said. She looked at me. "Hello, Tom." Then she turned to her brother. "Joe, could you take Mr. Derringer's hat and put on the kettle?"

"*Where is he?*" Mrs. Vanderhart repeated, staring me in the eye.

"Wildwood Island," I said, as I handed the lad my hat. "I take it you got my telegram."

"We did," Betsy said, as her mother glared wordlessly at me. "You said you would explain."

"And I will! I assure you, it is in no way as bad as we feared. Your father and the other missing scientists are alive and well, safe and well fed and in no immediate danger." I gestured at a chair. "Might I sit down?"

"Please," Betsy said, dragging her mother by force back to her own just-abandoned chair.

When all three of us were seated I began, "Professor Vanderhart is currently in the employ of an eccentric and very wealthy Frenchman by the name of Sebastien Boireau."

"*Employ?* He teaches at the college!" Mrs. Vanderhart exclaimed.

"But I believe he is presently on sabbatical?"

"Yes, he is," Betsy confirmed. "He took the year off to visit that volcano in the South Seas, Krakatoa or whatever it's called. What does that have to do with anything?"

"Since he had returned to America but would not be resuming classes until the fall, Monsieur Boireau hired him as a researcher - presumably just until September, though I do not know all the details and have my doubts about whether Monsieur Boireau will abide by his agreements."

"But he was *kidnapped!*" Mrs. Vanderhart burst out.

I nodded. "He was, yes. Mr. de la Rue had been sent to hire him, and when the professor proved reluctant, de la Rue resorted to force to bring him to Monsieur Boireau for further discussion.

De la Rue's employer does not readily take no for an answer. I do not know exactly what methods of persuasion were brought to bear, but in the end the professor agreed to accept the position. He was told that you, Mrs. Vanderhart, would be informed by messenger of what had happened; he was horrified to learn that no such message was ever delivered."

"You spoke to him? He told you this?"

"I did, yes, and the expression on his face when I told him you had had no word from him was..." I shook my head and left the sentence unfinished. "He has been writing to you regularly, but his letters have been intercepted. He had thought the lack of response was because you were angry with him, not because his letters were not received."

"This Monsieur Boireau sounds like someone who can't be trusted," Betsy said.

"Indeed, I would say he is something of a villain, though he fancies himself a hero defending civilization from a great threat."

"What kind of a *hero* would hold a prisoner incommunicado, leaving his family with no idea what had become of him?" Betsy demanded.

"An obsessive and perhaps somewhat deranged one," I replied.

"But *why?*" Mrs. Vanderhart wailed. "Why keep us so completely in the dark? Why not let his letters reach us?"

"Because Monsieur Boireau is obsessed with secrecy," I said. "He is absolutely certain that his enemies have spies everywhere, and he does not want a single living soul outside his own establishments to have any idea what he's up to. He fears that even his own employees cannot be trusted, that the professor's letters might either inadvertently or deliberately reveal things he does not want known. If he finds out that I have visited his camp on Wildwood and am now roaming free with a fairly good idea of his plans, he would probably send his men to find me and either capture or kill me." I had come to this conclusion on the train ride north, but had never before put it into words spoken aloud; I did not know just how far Boireau would go to keep his intentions hidden, but I had to admit that assassins were not entirely out of the question.

"Would it really have been so dreadful to at least *tell* us what became of my husband?"

I could only spread my hands. "I can't speak for him," I said. "I don't know exactly what his thinking on the matter is."

"All right," Betsy said. "Tell us what you *do* know."

"You realize, I trust, that by revealing his secrets to you, I may be endangering *you*, as well?"

"Then tell us only what you feel safe," Betsy said.

I nodded, and began, "Monsieur Boireau believes that the entire civilized world will soon be facing a threat from a mysterious group of a completely unknown nature. They may be human, or they may not, but they have resources unlike anything known to modern science. In order to oppose them, Monsieur Boireau has established several enclaves, scattered around the world, where scientists are researching ways to resist these invaders when they do finally reveal themselves and attack us."

"Invaders?" Betsy asked. "What *sort* of invaders?"

"I believe that is one of the secrets it is better you do not know."

"Go on," Mrs. Vanderhart said.

"There are two of these enclaves in the United States," I said. "One is somewhere in the northwest, on the Pacific coast, and one is on Wildwood Island, here in New Jersey, just to the northeast of Cape May. In the course of my investigation of Professor Vanderhart's disappearance I learned that something strange might be happening on Wildwood Island. I went to see just what it might be, and found Monsieur Boireau's establishment there."

I described how I had seen the domes from my chartered boat and had swum and waded ashore; how I had explored the exterior, and then climbed the wall, and what I had seen there; and how I had by great good fortune happened upon Professor Vanderhart himself in fairly short order. I recounted some of our conversation, but I did not make any mention of the Lost City of the Mirage, nor did I explain the nature of the professor's research.

Somewhere in there Joe brought in a tray of tea, set it on a table, and then stood quietly in the background, listening. I made no objection to his presence, but continued my tale.

And at last, I described how we had confirmed our mutual suspicion that the professor was being held prisoner – a very comfortable and well–paid prisoner, but a prisoner nonetheless – and how I had then departed, regrouped at the Hotel Chalfonte, and come to see them.

After no more than three seconds of silence, Betsy got directly to the point: "How do we get him out?"

"I'm not sure yet," I said. "I had thought that it was obviously illegal to hold him against his will, but then I realized I don't know whether he might have signed a contract of some kind requiring him to remain there for some period of time. The law can be very generous with employers' rights, and I didn't think to ask him before I left."

"Well, go back and ask him!" Mrs. Vanderhart replied.

I shook my head. "Whether the law is on our side or not – and I rather suspect it is – I don't believe that Messrs. Boireau and de la Rue would be much troubled by that. The only law officer with jurisdiction on Wildwood Island is the sheriff of Cape May County, and while I have no doubt that the voters have chosen a brave and worthy man, I would not expect him to face down a dozen or more armed guards in order to enter a private fortress and remove a single man. Nor do I think Boireau's men would cooperate."

"Surely the sheriff could call for assistance somewhere!" Betsy said.

"Probably; I really don't know what the rules are. The little legal training I had did not concern itself with such things, but rather with the more common hazards of the adventurer's trade – mostly how to avoid charges of trespassing, assault, grave-robbing, and so on."

Both women started to protest, and I held up a hand.

"Remember," I said, "I *am* a trained adventurer. Rescuing prisoners is very much in my purview. I just say that we may not be able to march in with the sheriff and a judge's writ and have the professor handed over to us, so we must consider our options. I'm afraid that if we bring in law enforcement officers making demands the situation may turn violent, and that violence in close proximity to all the experimental equipment in that compound might end very badly indeed. That place is built entirely of wood and appears to be quite inflammable."

"Very well, Tom," Betsy said. "What *are* our options?"

"Well, one possibility would be to extract your father surreptitiously – perhaps cut a hole in the wall, escort him to a waiting boat, and carry him away. The problem I see in this is that once his absence is noted, and I cannot say with any assurance whether that would take minutes or months, Boireau's people would come looking for him and would undoubtedly come *here.* Unless you want to go into hiding, all of you, or live under constant guard, that would be awkward."

Mrs. Vanderhart frowned.

"Another possibility would be to convince Monsieur Boireau to release him," I said. "That may not be as difficult as one might assume. I do not think that Professor Vanderhart's research is essential to Boireau's efforts; it's really rather peripheral to his central objective."

"But he might just abduct *you,*" Betsy said. "Didn't you say he was behind the disappearances of several adventurers?"

"He is, yes," I admitted. "I have no intention of simply walking into his office unprepared, I assure you. In fact, for once, I don't intend to do *anything* until I have made careful plans and considered several contingencies. Your father is in no immediate danger, and while I know you miss him, the best course is to investigate every avenue before choosing one."

"I want my husband back!" Mrs. Vanderhart exclaimed.

"And you shall have him, I promise! I am simply trying to find the best and safest way to go about it – safest for *him*, rather than for myself."

Betsy glared at her mother, then said, "Perhaps, Tom, you should get on with your schemes, then – unless there is something important you haven't told us?"

"I have done my best not to reveal the matters Monsieur Boireau wishes to keep secret, but other than that, I think I have covered all the essentials." I rose. "And my next step is to catch a train to New York, so that I can confer with my colleagues."

Betsy leapt to her feet. "Colleagues?"

"My fellow adventurers – some of them undoubtedly have past experience with situations similar enough to this that their advice will be helpful. As I said, I do not want to undertake this venture alone."

"But how do you know who you can trust? What if some of them are on Monsieur Boireau's payroll?"

"Oh, I think..." I began.

"I'm coming with you," she interrupted.

"What?"

"I'm coming with you," she repeated.

I considered that for a moment. I always welcomed Betsy's company – not just because she was a charming young woman whose presence brightened any surroundings, but because she was smart and resourceful and often displayed greater common sense than I did myself. However, this affair might well prove dangerous, and I did not want to put her at risk unnecessarily.

"Are you sure?" I said.

"I am."

"You do not think you need to stay to look after your mother?"

Betsy glanced at Mrs. Vanderhart, who I noticed was not participating in the discussion. "My mother can take care of herself, Tom, and if she can't, Joe and Dirk can look after her."

"I'll be fine," Mrs. Vanderhart said. "If it will get my Al back home any quicker, then by all means, Elspeth, you go help."

"Let me get my things," she said.

I was not inclined to argue. I sat and drank my tea, chatting with Joe – attempts to bring Mrs. Vanderhart into the conversation did not fare well – for perhaps fifteen minutes, until Betsy reappeared with a carpetbag in hand and said, "Let's go, Tom."

This carpetbag was not the luggage she had brought with her during our adventures out West; it appeared to be in better condition than any baggage I had seen her use before. I did not comment on it, but merely picked up my own bag and umbrella. I found my hat on the coat rack, and retrieved that, as well.

Betsy paused to kiss her mother on the forehead and told her brother, "Take care of everything, Joe." Then we were out the door and on our way to the railroad station, with Mrs. Vanderhart calling admonitions to be careful after us.

Once the door had closed behind us, Betsy let out a great sigh. "Thank you, Tom," she said. "Living with my mother and without my father was driving me mad."

"It was your choice to stay," I pointed out.

"Yes, it was, and I don't regret it. From your account I do not think my presence would have been any help at all in your recent adventures, and if you will forgive me for saying so, I really needed some time away from you."

"I understand," I said – not because I did entirely understand, but because it seemed the best answer available.

"It was good to spend time with Mother, at least at first; we were able to comfort each other and share our worries about

Father. We were able to put our differences behind us, at least partially – she seems to be over her bout of religious mania, but she has not entirely let go of her concern over the fact that I killed a man."

"Has she..."

Betsy did not allow me to finish my question. "She has not openly accused me of anything, but she has managed to mention more than once that *she* never killed anyone."

"Well, I don't suppose most people *have* killed anyone," I said.

"I suppose not," she admitted.

"You know, I am not certain whether I have ever said this, but I am most heartily sorry, Betsy, for putting you in a situation where your best available course of action was to shoot someone."

"*That* is hardly the worst situation you have put me in, Tom! Have you forgotten the months spent as prisoners of the lizard people?"

"Not at all! But I think there is rather a difference between the two." I hesitated, trying to think how I might best explain the difference, then concluded that there was no need to. Betsy surely knew what I meant.

We continued some distance in silence, but my thoughts on our adventures together turned to another point. I knew better than to ask why she had willingly accompanied me in the past, but the present remained an open question. "If you really wish to avoid such misadventures, why are you here?" I asked. "Surely there are other ways to escape the discomforts of home and hearth."

"I suppose there are," she said, "but this one presented itself – and I *do* want to help you get my father back safely. Besides, you say you will not act rashly, even though in all the time I have known you that is exactly what you have repeatedly done, but even if you abide by that assurance I am concerned that you may put your faith in the wrong people. You admit that this Monsieur Boireau has agents scattered about, and I think I may be of service in helping you to avoid trusting them."

That, I realized, was precisely what I had hoped to hear.

"Good," I said.

And then we were at the station and turned our attention to schedules and fares.

Chapter Thirteen

Exploring My Options

We transferred at the Pennsylvania Railroad Station in Jersey City and boarded our ferry into New York. From Courtland Street I had intended to return once again to the Robertson Hotel, but Betsy had other plans.

"My father maintains a flat on East Eighteenth Street," Betsy said. "I use it whenever I have business in New York, and I see no reason we should not do so on this occasion. I have brought the keys with me. There are two bedrooms, so we need commit no impropriety."

That was obviously the superior option – it would render me more difficult to find, should any of Monsieur Boireau's minions be looking for me, and it would save me the cost of a hotel room, which I thought my mother and Toby Arbuthnot would appreciate. I quickly agreed and flagged down a hack; Betsy gave him an address, the Portman Hotel, though she explained afterward that it was not, in fact, where we would be staying, but stood across the street perhaps half a block to the west of our actual destination. I thought this might be an excess of caution, but then again, everyone involved in this adventure seemed to think spies were everywhere, and how could I be certain that they weren't?

The flat, on the third floor of five, was sparsely furnished, but comfortable enough. The kitchen held no food but a few canned vegetables – unsurprising, given how irregularly the place was occupied – which meant we would be eating our meals elsewhere. The beds, however, were properly made up, and the pleasantly modern bathroom was equipped with half a dozen towels. The professor obviously intended this establishment to serve as a mere stopover, rather than a long–term residence, but that was precisely what we needed. We took an hour or so to rest after our journey and settle in, and then set out for Mad Bill Snedeker's Perry Street tavern.

I made some desultory attempt to convince Betsy that our destination was not a suitable establishment for a lady, but I knew I would not be able to discourage her, and therefore did not waste much time on the effort.

It was late afternoon when we arrived at Snedeker's Tavern & Billiard Emporium, and I believe Betsy might have had some second thoughts when she got her first look at the interior, but of course she would not admit to any such a thing. She followed me inside without hesitation.

Mr. Dobbs was manning the bar, as usual; I walked up and asked, "Is Mr. Snedeker in?"

"Mr. Derringer? He expecting you?" He glanced past me. "Or the young lady?"

"No, I'm afraid we did not inform him we were coming. Is he in?"

"Just a moment." He set his towel down, emerged from behind the bar, and vanished into the back room.

I turned and leaned against the bar, looking out at the shabby little pool hall; Betsy turned as well, and took my arm as she eyed the unsavory few customers – half seated at one of the tables, and half playing pocket billiards. At least one of the billiard players was returning Betsy's gaze with a predatory expression while waiting his turn to shoot. I pointedly returned his glare.

Then Mr. Dobbs reappeared. "Go ahead," he said, as he returned to his duties.

"Thank you," I said, and I led Betsy through the open door.

Mad Bill Snedeker was seated in his customary place at the table that served as his desk; he started to speak, and then saw Betsy following me into the room. He immediately pushed back his chair and got to his feet, reaching for an imaginary hat to doff in the presence of a lady.

"Damme, Tom, who's this?" he asked.

"Uncle Bill, this is Elspeth Vanderhart. Betsy, this is William Snedeker, the owner of this establishment and a good friend to my late father."

"Pleased to meet you, sir," Betsy said, with a slight curtsy. She could not help staring.

I did not blame her. Mad Bill Snedeker was roughly as fat as Betsy's own father, so I don't suppose his size greatly startled her, but he was possessed of a truly prodigious gray–streaked beard that rivaled – nay, surpassed! – in volume her own magnificent blonde curls. I have never seen it bettered by any man.

"And I am absolutely *delighted* to meet you, my dear!" he replied. "Tom, what's this about? Why have you brought this precious flower into a dive like mine?" His expression changed. "Is this the friend whose father was carried off?"

I nodded. "She is. The good news, Uncle Bill, is that I found him, and he's alive and well."

"And how the devil does this bring the both of you *here*?"

"Well, that's the other news. He's being held against his will, and I hoped I might draw on your experience for advice."

"And Miss Vanderhart?"

"She asked to accompany me. She may have useful insights about her father to offer."

"Huh." He sat down again and glanced at an empty beer mug near his elbow. "Would either of you care for a drink? I'm afraid I don't have much that would be suitable for a lady's more refined tastes, but..."

"I'll have a beer," Betsy interrupted.

"As will I," I said – and as I did, it occurred to me that we had not eaten since breakfast. "And do you suppose Mr. Dobbs could manage a sandwich or two?"

"Of course he could!" He rose to his feet and bellowed, "Dobbs! Get in here!"

The long-suffering Mr. Dobbs appeared in the doorway, and Mad Bill barked, "Three beers and a plate of sandwiches, and hurry!"

"Any particular sort of sandwiches?"

"Whatever we have. The *best* of whatever we have."

Mr. Dobbs vanished again.

"So," Mad Bill said, "tell me all about it."

I did.

It took quite some time, especially as I paused occasionally to take a swig of beer or bite into one of the magnificent roast beef sandwiches Mr. Dobbs had delivered. Having given the matter some thought, I had decided that this time I would hold back none of the details of Monsieur Boireau's plans and theories, so that some of the narrative was as new to Betsy as it was to Mad Bill.

At last I concluded with, "And here we are. Did I miss anything you want to know?"

"You missed something *I* want to know, Tom," Betsy said. "Where did you get this wonderful mustard, Mr. Snedeker?"

"I'll show you sometime, and call me Bill. Right now, though, I'd say we need to focus on how to get your father out of there."

"Getting him out isn't really that big a challenge," I said. "It's getting him out without sending Monsieur Boireau into fits and causing us a lot of trouble."

"That's the hard part, yes," Mad Bill agreed. "When we were all adventuring with Darien Lord we generally just got out of whatever part of the world we'd been making trouble in and came home, but this Boireau's operating right here in New York and New Jersey."

"He's operating all over the world, Uncle Bill!"

"I'm pretty damn sure there are places he hasn't got anything going on, but I can't say as to where they are, or whether you'd want to live in any of 'em."

"It seems to me," Betsy said, "that we should put an end to Monsieur Boireau's little empire. If he's holding my father prisoner, how many of his other employees may be there against their will? It's kidnapping, at the very least! He should be in prison!"

"He probably should," I agreed. "But he's very wealthy man, and I doubt we can convince the authorities to take him on without far more reason and evidence than we can provide."

"Tom's got it," Mad Bill agreed. "From what he says, it'd take a small army to capture this island of his by force, and the law there just has a sheriff with maybe a few deputies."

"We might see if Detective Morris, of the New Brunswick police, can provide any assistance."

"It's outside his jurisdiction."

"But the original kidnapping took place in his city."

"I'm not sure that would be enough. And didn't you say he couldn't be trusted?"

"Well, Betsy thought he might be on Boireau's payroll, but we don't have any real evidence of that..."

Before Bill could reply, Betsy interrupted, "Couldn't we hire the Pinkertons?"

Her suggestion caught me off guard; I had not considered this. Mrs. Vanderhart had rejected the idea of hiring them as detectives, but perhaps they might be useful in this situation. I looked at Mad Bill.

"If we had the money, we might," he said. "They charge eight dollars per man per day, plus expenses."

"I might have..." I began, though I knew the family finances were already somewhat strained.

Bill raise a hand. "Don't you go figuring it out yet, Tommy," he said. "We don't know how many men we would need, or whether they'd take the job. Hell, Boireau may already have hired them! Where'd those guards of his come from?"

I had not considered that, either, but when I gave it some thought I had to agree it was not merely possible, but fairly likely. Mrs. Vanderhart's suspicions might well prove correct. "We would need to look into that," I said.

"He could get men who'd work cheaper, no question, but if he wanted people he could *trust*...well, in his position I'd at least *talk* to the Pinkertons."

"He seems to spend pretty freely," I said. "I don't think the cost would deter him. So those *might* be Pinkertons."

"Then we should hire someone else!" Betsy said.

"I don't know," I replied. "Even if we found someone else doing that sort of work, it might lead to bloodshed."

"A damned great deal of bloodshed, I'd say, if Boireau's men decide to fight."

"Why would they fight?" Betsy demanded. "If the law says they're wrong, and there are armed men telling them to surrender, and they're outnumbered, why would they still resist?"

Bill and I exchanged looks. "Because that's what some men *do*," I said patiently.

"Especially when they're being paid to," Bill added.

"And we can't be sure they'd be outnumbered," I said, "unless we bring a veritable army. We don't even know whether most of the scientists consider themselves prisoners – Boireau is paying them generously. What's more, he's paying them to invent *weapons* – electrical weapons. We don't know what we might be up against; it might not just be guns."

"Damme, hadn't thought of that," Bill muttered.

"And as I told your mother, Betsy, that compound of his looks tremendously inflammable."

No one cared to reply to that.

For a moment we sat quietly. Then I pushed aside my plate, dusted the last crumbs from my fingers, and said, "I had come here today in hopes that you might have had some experience that would give us a model to work from, Uncle Bill, but it sounds as if you're just as much at sea as we are."

"I'm afraid so. I like to think I'm no fool, but I was never the brains of our band, Tom – that was Mr. Lord, or when he wasn't available it might be Big Josh, or one of your parents, or even Smoky Ash, but it wasn't ever me. I had my wild ways, and I could sometimes look at things in ways no one else did, which is why I was called Mad Bill, but I wasn't ever the clever one. Neither was Candy Cal, either, despite what he thought, and some of our worst trouble came when he wouldn't listen to Josh." He shook his head. "I wish Josh were still with us."

"What happened to him?" Betsy asked.

"Froze to death in '73," Bill replied.

"In Russia," I added. "Siberia, I think. He was trying to stop an attempt to assassinate the Tsar."

"He *did* stop it," Bill pointed out. "It wasn't 'til eight years later that someone finally took Alexander down."

I nodded. Mad Bill stared morosely into the last few drops of his beer, then looked up and bellowed, "Dobbs!"

I pushed back my chair. "I think perhaps we should be going, Uncle Bill."

"All right," he said. "It's been a pleasure to meet you, Miss Vanderhart, and you feel free to stop by any time you like – first drink's on the house."

Mr. Dobbs had appeared in the doorway, and Mad Bill held up his empty mug.

"You, too, Tom." he said, as Mr. Dobbs vanished again. "You come by whenever the whim strikes you; you don't need an excuse. And let me know if there's anything I can do to help that doesn't involve real thinking, as that was never my strong suit."

"Oh, Mr. Snedeker..." Betsy protested.

"Don't mind me. I'm just getting a little gloomy thinking about old friends I'll never see again," he said. "Tom, you come around sometimes; I don't want to miss any *new* friends."

I wondered just how many mugs of beer he had drunk before we arrived. "I'll do that, Uncle Bill, just as soon as we've got Professor Vanderhart safely back home." I held out a hand and waited while he moved his mug to his left; we shook, and then I turned to go, just as Mr. Dobbs returned with another beer.

Out on the street we turned our footsteps to the east; for the first hundred yards Betsy said nothing, glancing frequently back over her shoulder, but then she asked, "Where are we going next?"

"To visit the Order of Theseus," I said.

"The adventurers' guild?"

"They don't...it's not exactly that," I said. "It's a club that limits its membership to proven adventurers, yes, but there are plenty of adventurers who never join, and the Order makes no attempt to organize or regulate anyone. It's purely a social organization, not a guild."

"Are you a member?"

"Not yet," I said. "I have put in my name, and I have been nominated and seconded, but I don't believe they've voted yet, and I haven't been initiated. But they've made me welcome as a guest." We turned left onto Seventh Avenue at the next corner.

It was about a twenty-minute walk to the Order's headquarters; I suppose we could have hired a hack, but I was glad to breathe the fresh air after spending an hour or so in the stuffy confines of Mad Bill's back room, and a chance to think was also welcome.

I had expected Betsy to have some things to say about our situation, but to my surprise she did not say a word. I noticed she did seem to be keeping a wary eye out, and I wondered whether she was worried that Monsieur Boireau's agents might be eavesdropping on us.

If they were, they were being quite subtle. I was somewhat more wary than I usually am when on familiar streets in New York, and I did not notice a single person who seemed to be paying us any attention. We arrived at the Order's door without incident.

The big bronze door was locked, of course, and I did not yet have a key, but I knew how to find the concealed bell–pull, and upon ringing it a panel behind what appeared to be a ventilation grille in the left–hand wall of the portico slid open.

No one spoke from the darkness thus revealed, but I addressed the opening.

"My name is Derringer, J. Thomas Derringer. I'd like to speak to whichever members might be available."

"Is this regarding an offer of employment, or a request for assistance?" a woman's voice asked.

"Not employment," I said, "but it may involve a request for assistance. For the most part I'm looking for advice."

The voice did not speak again, but a click sounded, and the bronze door opened a crack. I pushed it wide and led Betsy into the rather grandiose anteroom beyond.

Chapter Fourteen

We Consult with An Adventurer

We stood in the center of the anteroom, waiting; the normal procedure was for an unaccompanied guest to wait there for one or more members to admit him to the rooms beyond. I had seen this antechamber before, but Betsy had not, and she looked around at the elaborate decorations with interest. I pointed out the mummy case in the corner and said, "That's genuine; I'm told it dates to Egypt's Middle Kingdom. The medieval armor opposite, though, is a modern recreation."

"Yes, it is," that same woman's voice replied, "but it was used in an elaborate fraud meant to bring down the Bank of England. It failed, of course, thanks to some of our members." The speaker appeared in an archway to our left. "Mr. Derringer? I'm Sarah Darlington."

She was not someone I recalled seeing before. She was tall and slender, perhaps no more than an inch shorter than my own five feet and eleven inches, with hair a peculiar shade of pale blonde. She wore a high-collared dark blue dress with an unfashionably modest bustle and no jewelry or other such adornment. She strode up to us and held out a hand. I took it, unsure whether she meant me to kiss it, or merely shake hands. I chose the latter, and that seemed to please her. "A pleasure to meet you, Miss Darlington," I said. "I'm Tom Derringer, and my companion is Miss Elspeth Vanderhart."

"Miss Darlington," Betsy acknowledged.

"Darlington," I said. "Any relation to Mr. Ashton Darlington?"

"My father," she said. "And of course, I know who *your* father was."

"Of course." Ashton Darlington, known to his friends as Smoky Ash, had, like Mad Bill Snedeker, been one of my father's companions in Darien Lord's band; he had vanished somewhere in Africa many years earlier. I had not known he had a daughter; in fact, I knew almost nothing about him beyond what my father had said in his journals. I knew he had been married, but had not remembered any mention of children.

Of course, given Miss Darlington's apparent age, she might not have been born yet when Mr. Lord's group disbanded in 1861.

"Now, Mr. Derringer, what brings you to the Order of Theseus? If this is in regard to your application for membership, I'm afraid I'm not authorized to tell you anything about it even if I knew, which I do not."

"No, of course; I mean, obviously I am curious about my status here, but I would not expect you to have any news. I will wait until I am officially notified."

"Then why *are* you here? What advice are you after?"

"I assume you know several scientists have gone missing in recent months. I am in a somewhat delicate position regarding them. I hoped to confer with more experienced adventurers regarding my best course of action."

"Ah." She looked around, then said, "Come with me."

We obeyed, and she led us through an unfamiliar door, down a passage, and into a small wood-paneled room I had never seen before, where, at her suggestion, we took seats around a table. I was puzzled by this, but cooperated.

"Now," she said, once we were settled, "what's this about missing scientists?"

"I would have assumed you knew that several scientists have gone missing in recent months."

"Of course I know that! And half a dozen adventurers, as well, though the authorities refuse to take that part seriously."

"Miss Vanderhart's father is one of those scientists," I said. "She asked me to find him."

"Yes?" She glanced at Betsy, who said nothing, then turned her attention back to me. "Are you looking for assistance in this search? I assure you several members of the Order have already taken an interest in the matter."

"No, Miss Darlington; I would not simply walk in here unannounced for such assistance. I know where to find that sort of help should I need it. However, I have, in fact, *found* Professor Vanderhart and at least some of the other scientists, and I have a pretty good idea where the adventurers are, as well. What I am after is a way to free the professor without repercussions, given that his captors have extensive resources, and I cannot be sure of who can be trusted. In fact, I cannot be absolutely certain that *you* are not in the employ of his captor, and I am taking a risk by speaking to you."

"You found them?" She seemed startled – almost alarmed.

"Well, many of them, at any rate."

"How?"

"That's a rather long story and not really important right now. What's important is finding a way of getting Professor Vanderhart safely home without bloodshed."

"Would you care to explain that?"

I sighed. "Professor Vanderhart and the others were not exactly kidnapped. They were *hired* by a certain person. Some were abducted initially, but some went voluntarily, and all, so far as I know, eventually consented to employment – the salary offered was extraordinarily generous. However, because the work they were hired to perform is secret, their employer has allowed absolutely no communication with the outside world; attempts to contact friends or family have been frustrated at every turn, and their employer has lied to them, telling them that their families are aware of their situation. Which, of course, they are not. Although many of them continue to accept what they are told and do not yet realize it, these employees are now being confined to their hidden laboratories, guarded by...well, I'm not sure just who the guards are. Adventurers, perhaps, or Pinkertons, or simply hired thugs."

"Confined?"

I nodded. "When Professor Vanderhart attempted to depart, he was told in no uncertain terms that he would not be permitted to leave the compound."

"Really. And you could see no way to free him?"

"Oh, don't be ridiculous!" Betsy exclaimed before I could reply. "Of course Tom could get him out. But if he came home, this...this *person* would send his minions after him!"

"Or so we assume," I added hastily. "Given the man's obsession with secrecy, and his conviction that his foes have spies everywhere, I find it hard to believe he would accept the professor's departure as a *fait accompli*."

"If they are being held against their will, can you call on the local authorities, wherever they are?"

I shook my head. "I do not know whether that would do any good. Miss Darlington, if you will forgive me, I did not come here specifically to talk to *you* – while you are, I am sure, despite your youth, a knowledgeable and experienced adventurer, I hoped to get *several* viewpoints and suggestions." I gestured at our surroundings. "I'm not entirely sure why you brought me here instead of the main lobby."

"Because, Mr. Derringer, when I said that several members of the Order have taken an interest in the matter of the missing scientists, I was including myself. I hoped that perhaps we might form an alliance to pursue the investigation without involving the entire Order. If you might take me into your confidence regarding this mysterious employer, and the whereabouts of the missing men..."

"No!" Betsy snapped, leaping to her feet. "We don't know you. For all we know, you could be in that Frenchman's pay!"

"Frenchman?"

Betsy realized she had let something slip and immediately sat back down, lips tightly sealed.

"My companion spoke hastily," I said, "but she has an excellent point. While your father and mine were friends who trusted each other with their lives, I do not know you; I never met you before today, and know nothing about you. I do not even have proof that you are who you claim to be; until a few minutes ago I was unaware that Ashton Darlington was reported to have any children, and I still cannot be sure that he truly did. Your entire identity could be a ruse. We know that some adventurers are indeed in the employ of the man responsible for Professor Vanderhart's present situation; how can we be sure you aren't one of them, looking to confound our efforts to free him?"

"And how do *I* know that this mysterious figure has not sent *you* here to send us off on a wild goose chase? You claim to know where the missing scientists are being held – well, where is it?"

"Tom, we should not have come," Betsy said. "If she *is* working for...for him, and tells him we know, he might move all the prisoners!"

I was struck dumb by this suggestion; how could I have failed to consider this?

But then I realized that relocating all those men and their equipment was not something that could be done quickly and easily. Even if Miss Darlington were to leave the room and head directly to meet with Monsieur Boireau in his office on Hudson Street, we would surely still have at least a day or two to free the professor.

"I am not working for whoever is holding those men prisoner," Miss Darlington said. "I was hired by Aubrey Elliot's sister to find him and bring him safely home."

I exchanged a glance with Betsy. "I know Mr. Elliot is among the missing," I said.

"You are free to wire Mrs. Stallings and ask her yourself."

"We may do that," I said. "Once we confirm that Aubrey Elliot *has* a sister named Stallings, and obtain her address. You will understand we can't take your word for it."

"Dr. Pierce would know, wouldn't he?" Betsy said.

"I would assume so, yes."

"Dr. Pierce? The archivist?"

"Yes, of course. I assume you have consulted him?"

She shook her head. "I'm afraid I cannot afford his fees. But let us assume for now, Mr. Derringer, that the three of us are all telling the truth; can you tell me whether Mr. Elliot is one of the captives you found?"

"I regret to say I cannot. In the compound where the captives are being held I spoke only with Professor Vanderhart, and he did not mention Mr. Elliot's name."

"But of course, you can't trust a word we say, any more than we can trust you," Betsy pointed out.

Miss Darlington glared sourly at her; Betsy stared defiantly back.

"Tom," Betsy continued, "we can't trust *anyone* here! Half the Order might be in...in *his* pay."

I could not argue with that, but I said, "Perhaps we can find a way to recruit the *other* half."

"Only if we find a way to identify them."

"Who *is* this man?" Miss Darlington demanded.

"A man who believes he is saving civilization," I said. "He has put all these men to work developing defenses against an enemy I am fairly certain is imaginary."

"And he has the resources to hide away dozens of scientists and adventurers and hire guards to watch over them?"

"He does," I said. "He's fabulously wealthy. And he has

been planning this for years."

"A wealthy Frenchman with delusions about a threat to all of civilization?"

"We've said too much," Betsy said.

A thought struck me. "Or not enough," I said. "He's been desperate to keep his operations secret, so that his supposed foes will be caught unprepared when they finally launch their assault and find themselves confronted by his electrical empire, but suppose we were to reveal *all* his secrets and spread the word as widely as we can? Then he would have no need to keep his scientists sequestered in his private compounds."

"You'd be taking quite a risk," Miss Darlington said. "Is he the sort of person who would accept such a revelation, or one who would seek revenge against the parties responsible? You might be inviting your own murder. And he might try to keep secret anything you do *not* reveal – surely, he has secrets you do not know?"

"I'm sure he does," I admitted. "Certainly, I know nothing of the technical details of the devices his employees have created."

"I'm not sure I see how this would work out," Betsy said. "And...and I know this is unlikely, Tom, but what if he's *right* about the Lost...about the threat? Wouldn't we be ruining our own best hope of defense against the threatened invasion by interfering with his plans?"

"If he's right, Miss Vanderhart," Miss Darlington said, "shouldn't *everyone* be preparing defenses, and not a single wealthy madman?"

"Well, if he's right, is he truly mad?" Betsy countered.

"I don't think he's right," I said. "The logic doesn't work. There's something mysterious going on, certainly, but I don't think his explanation makes any sense. And even if it should have a kernel of truth, we have no way of knowing *when* the attack might come – your father says that even if it's real, which he does not believe to be the case, it might not happen for decades, perhaps a century. Should these men live out the rest of their lives isolated from civilization, cut off from their families, waiting for it?"

Betsy shuddered. "I want my father back."

"I wish you would tell me what's going on," Miss Darlington said. "What sort of an attack are we talking about? Who is this Frenchman? What does he want with those scientists? Where is he keeping them?"

I sighed. "Miss Darlington, if you are indeed working for...for the Frenchman, you almost certainly already know the answers to those questions. If you *aren't*, then telling you would put you in danger..."

"Only if he finds out you've told me," she interrupted.

"You told *me*," Betsy said. "You told Bill."

"I *know* you," I said, "and I know Uncle Bill. I've only just met Miss Darlington." I shook my head. "Coming here was a mistake. I can't trust the Order."

"Tom, maybe you *should* tell everyone about the entire thing," Betsy said.

"But then he'd be putting his *own* life at risk, if the Frenchman wants revenge," Miss Darlington replied.

That seemed to me as if she was undercutting her own position – she certainly wanted me to tell *her* everything I knew. But perhaps she had reasons for not wanting it widely disseminated. It might be that she really was working for Boireau, or it might merely be that she wanted to earn her fee for finding Aubrey Elliot before anyone else could set him free.

"Tom, you've spoken to the Frenchman," Betsy asked. "Do you think he's the vengeful sort?"

"I can't say," I answered. "I wouldn't put it past him."

"You know," Miss Darlington said, "you may not realize how much you have already told me. You say you know where the scientists are being held; do you think no one in the Order is capable of retracing your steps and finding them, as you did?

Miss Vanderhart says you have told *her* all the Frenchman's secrets, and likewise someone you call Uncle Bill. Perhaps you forget, Mr. Derringer, or never knew, that I grew up hearing stories of the adventures our fathers had together. I know Jack Derringer was a homeless orphan, with no known family, when Mr. Lord took him in, and surely it would not be difficult to find any brothers that Arabella Whitaker may have had. Should I actually be in the Frenchman's pay, you have *already* put their lives in danger. You are fortunate that I am not."

For a moment, no one spoke; then Betsy said, "That was unforgivably careless of me. I'm sorry, Tom."

"I didn't do any better." I was thinking hard. "All right, Miss Darlington," I said. "I am not going to reveal any more secrets just now. You're probably right that I've told you enough that you can follow my path and find the Frenchman's compound, though I don't know whether Aubrey Elliot is among the men held there. That means that unless I dissuade you, whatever I am going to do must be done fairly quickly, before you can locate the place and take action on your own. I can think of no good means to dissuade you, and in fact I am not sure I *want* to. I would suggest as a strategy, however, that you recruit any other members of the Order you can ascertain to have been hired, as you were, to find one specific individual among the missing scientists, and work together with them to present a united front against the Frenchman's guards."

"And will you not join us in this effort? Will you not save us the trouble of retracing your path?"

I shook my head. "Not yet," I said. "Perhaps later."

"What if the Frenchman's agents discover our plans?"

"Then you may find yourself in an awkward position – which is why I will not join you immediately. Might I request that so far as possible, you do not mention my name?"

"I...damn you, Mr. Derringer, you are making this very awkward! Why cannot we simply work together?"

"Because," I said, "I have other approaches I wish to try."
And with that I rose, took Betsy's hand, and led her back out to
the street.

Chapter Fifteen

Preparations Are Made

Betsy did not say a word until we were not merely back on the street, but walking up the sidewalk around the corner from the entrance to the Order's headquarters.

"What other approaches?" she asked, at last.

"I'm afraid I don't want to tell you that right now," I replied.

She frowned. "I can see why you didn't want to tell Miss Darlington anything," she said. "We had already been careless, and she might pick up any hint we let slip, and we don't know yet whether she can be trusted. But why don't you want to tell *me* what you're planning?"

"You might try to stop me."

She stopped walking and grabbed my arm. "Tom, what are you thinking? What harebrained scheme are you hatching?"

"One that requires you to be safely out of sight," I replied.

"Well, I am not going to *stay* out of sight unless you tell me more than that! And where are we going?"

I sighed. "We are returning to your family's flat on Eighteenth Street. Am I correct in assuming that its existence is not widely known?"

"Oh, well...I don't know that I would say that. It's not secret. My father has met with some of his associates there, on occasion."

"What sort of associates?"

"Engineers, mostly, and other scientists. The same sort of people he sent me all over the country to meet with, regarding his projects."

"So they would know the address?"

"Yes."

"And your mother does?"

"Of course."

I frowned. "Perhaps you should stay with *my* mother instead, then."

"Your mother's address is not secret, either!"

"We try to limit knowledge of it to a few trusted friends, though we had to extend that circle somewhat when I was being schooled as an adventurer."

"You gave *me* your address on the ship from Belize Town and never said anything about that!"

"I had hoped you might write to me, and I certainly consider you a trusted friend."

"Oh," she said.

"That's at the heart of my plan, Betsy – that you are a trusted friend. As for where you might stay in my absence, should the Eighteenth Street residence prove unsatisfactory, Mad Bill might have a suggestion."

"What sort of suggestion?"

I did not answer her question directly. Instead I said, "I am going to attempt to strike a bargain with Monsieur Boireau. I expect to explain, in the course of negotiations, that I have revealed everything I know to certain trusted friends. I will not name names, but anyone who has followed my career as an adventurer at all, as Boireau has, will quickly guess that *you* are my dearest and most trusted friend. I have tried to downplay your part in our adventures, but I doubt I have managed to conceal it, especially when it's known that I am looking for your father. Should these negotiations with our adversary fail, I expect Boireau to try to find and silence the friends I have told, and he will certainly assume that you are one of them. In that eventuality I want you to be somewhere securely out of his reach. I am hoping that my connections to Mad Bill are not well enough known to put him at risk, but *you* – well, you are the obvious target. So I want you to go into hiding and stay well away from me for a time."

Her frown deepened. "I see."

"It occurs to me that it would be useful if you, in turn, were to explain the situation in detail to your own trusted friends – friends I do not know, and who have no connections with adventurers or scientists. That would provide a second line of defense."

"Most of my friends are back in New Brunswick, but...but I might have a few here in the city."

"Good! Don't tell me anything more."

"Of course not. So, Tom, how do you plan to conduct these negotiations? By post?"

I shook my head. "I don't think I should tell you," I said. "I will point out that there is an obvious problem with negotiating by letter."

"You'd need to give him an address, and even if you use general delivery, he can station men at the post office to wait for you."

"Yes. Obvious, as I said."

"So you'll tell him that you've told us everything – and then what?"

"Then he'll know that simply silencing *me* won't suffice to protect his secrets, and if I do not return in a reasonable time, you and Mad Bill will spread what you know far and wide, beginning with the police – the whereabouts of the missing men, the plans to build electrical devices to defend against invasion, everything."

"And you want me to spread it so that he won't think killing *me* will keep it quiet."

"Well, I was thinking more in terms of abduction rather than outright murder, but yes."

"Tom, if I spread it widely enough that he can't suppress it, it won't be much of a secret anymore."

I shrugged. "This does not trouble me. If he *thinks* it is still a secret, he won't risk taking action against me – or your father, once we have him safely back home. Whether it is *actually* secret – well, frankly, I don't care."

"Monsieur Boireau might."

"Let him. Oh, and Betsy, once we separate, if you could please tell Mad Bill to do the same as I have asked of you, and pass the story on to trustworthy friends, I would greatly appreciate it."

"*If* we separate. I don't think I like this plan."

"We are going to separate, and I am relying on you to tell Mad Bill what's happening."

"I don't like it."

"That does not surprise me. Nonetheless, I am going to try to bargain with Monsieur Boireau and convince him to release your father peacefully. I am asking you to help, but I intend to try this whether you agree to help or not, because every other approach I can think of has far too much risk of turning violent and endangering innocent lives."

For a moment she silently considered this, and then she nodded. "I will want to emphasize the *trustworthy* part, when I talk to Mr. Snedeker."

"Of course, but don't worry. Despite what he may tell you, Mad Bill Snedeker isn't stupid." I hesitated, as a memory struck me. "Or...well, you *will* want to emphasize the trustworthy part. He lost most of the money he made as an adventurer by trusting the wrong people when making investments. But he kept enough to buy his saloon, and for that matter he's stayed alive when most of his compatriots have not, so I hope he's learned better."

"I hope so, too."

With that, we resumed our journey. The conversation moved on to lighter matters, and not long after we arrived safely back at the flat on Eighteenth Street.

By this time it was late enough that I thought it best to put off any attempt to contact Monsieur Boireau until morning. We took a brief rest, then went out to do a little shopping, largely so that our kitchen would not be quite so empty. After that we dined at the Portman Tavern, just down the street from our flat. I had hoped that afterward we might go dancing, but I was unable, on such short notice and without the assistance of a hotel's staff, to locate a dance hall whose reputation was not a serious deterrent. In the end we abandoned the idea and instead took a casual stroll through Union Square Park.

At no time during this pleasant evening did we devote much attention to Monsieur Boireau and his plans, or to Professor Vanderhart's unhappy situation. Oh, these topics inevitably came up, but both of us were determined to put them aside for now, having established that I would pursue the matter on the morrow.

We did establish, though, that negotiation was not my *only* strategy, and that I did not consider our visit to the Order of Theseus to be a total loss. I fully expected Sarah Darlington to continue her own investigation, and, with the hints and provocations I had given her, to identify Sebastien Boireau as the man behind the disappearances, though it might take her a few days. Whether she located the compound on Wildwood Island I considered roughly an even-money bet, but either way I thought she would soon complicate Monsieur Boireau's life, giving us more to offer him in future negotiations.

We also discussed ways we might communicate while Betsy was in hiding, ways that could not be intercepted, and Betsy suggested a brilliant, if somewhat difficult, scheme – we would write any notes to one another in Kanta'an, the language of the lizard people who lived in tunnels beneath Los Angeles – the Skyless, as they called themselves. We had both learned it while imprisoned there; Betsy was far more fluent than I, as I did not have her knack for languages, but I knew enough to get by. We need have no worries that any intercepted notes would be read; in all probability the only people on Earth who knew that tongue were ourselves, a man named Gabriel Trask who at last report was on his way to the lost city of El Dorado, and the Skyless themselves.

That still left time for a few words of a purely personal nature. It was not long before midnight when we finally returned to our apartment and retired for the night in our separate bedrooms.

In the morning we ate breakfast together, but then I left Betsy to her own devices while I headed across town to Monsieur Boireau's office on Hudson Street. I *hoped* that Betsy would go talk to Mad Bill, but I had deliberately not asked her what her plans were; if asked, I could not tell anyone what I did not know.

I had no way of knowing whether Monsieur Boireau would be there, but I thought that at the very least I could leave a message; if no one was there at all I could slip a note under the door.

I had considered trying to contact Mr. de la Rue instead, but I had no idea whether he was still at the Hotel Brunswick; Monsieur Boireau might well have sent him to another city entirely on some errand, or after having delivered me for questioning, he might have returned to Cape May – or more likely, to the compound on Wildwood Island, as Professor Vanderhart had made it clear that de la Rue handled much of the day–to–day management there. I thought I would do better to go directly to Monsieur Boireau than to waste time at the Brunswick or, quite aside from the risks of giving an address, to suffer the inevitable delays of communicating through the mails.

The wind was cold, so I kept my coat pulled tight around me, and my hat pushed firmly down. The air was damp and the sky gray, but it was not actually raining. Spring did not seem to be in any hurry to assert itself this year.

I arrived at the building, entered, and climbed the stairs, and found one of Monsieur Boireau's bodyguards lounging beside the door of Room Four, his hat dangling from his left hand; I took this as an encouraging sign. I stepped past him and knocked.

He straightened up, clapped his hat on his head, and eyed me warily, but did not interfere.

A moment later the door opened, and another familiar face looked out at me.

"Mr. Cathcart," I said, tipping my own hat. "Is Monsieur Boireau in?"

"Mr. Derringer? May I ask what this is about?" I had not previously heard him speak, and I noticed he had a faint trace of a Scots accent.

"I have thought of something I should have told Monsieur Boireau during our interview," I said. "Given the generosity of his payment, and having nothing urgent planned for today, I thought I would stop in and see if he was interested."

"I'm afraid he is not here just now. If you'd like to tell me whatever it is, I can pass the message on to him."

"I'd really prefer to speak to him in person. Will he be in later, or perhaps tomorrow?"

Mr. Cathcart hesitated, looked at the guard, then turned back to me and said, "I don't know his schedule, but if you could come back this afternoon around three, I should be able to tell you more."

"Thank you, sir; I will be back around three, then." I tipped my hat, and left.

As it was not yet ten, that left me with more than four hours to fill. I stopped by a newsstand and picked up the day's *New York World*; I had heard that the paper had changed ownership while I was in California, and was curious as to whether there had been any remarkable alterations to its reporting. I could not see any, but then, I had hardly been a regular reader before the purchase. It was perhaps somewhat more restrained in its partisanship than I remembered, but not so much that I found it noteworthy.

I read through it as I walked crosstown to the Pierce Archives. I had come to the realization that if some *other* adventurer – Sarah Darlington, for example – were to bring about the collapse of Monsieur Boireau's empire, then Professor Vanderhart would be free to return home without any risk of retaliation. With that in mind, I intended to make it as easy as possible to follow in my footsteps without actually *telling* anyone where I had gone or what I had done. Perhaps someone else more ingenious than myself, or with greater resources, might bring the entire enterprise down without any risk to me or my friends.

Accordingly, I stopped in at the Archives and spoke with Dr. Pierce, telling him that while I still trusted him to be discreet, my previous visit was *not* to be considered confidential, and he was free to mention my interest in de la Rue and Boireau to anyone who asked.

I also asked whether there was anything I should know about Sarah Darlington.

"Eldest of Ashton Darlington's three children," he told me. "I have never met her, but I am told she is quite a striking young woman. She took up adventuring after her father's disappearance, when she was not yet twenty; neither of her brothers, nor her mother, saw fit to pursue the matter, believing the trail to be cold, but Miss Darlington spent her entire inheritance and the better part of three years in attempting to retrace, with the help of assorted adventurers, her father's steps from the Sultan's palace in Morocco to the unexplored regions of the African continent. She lost the trail somewhere in the Adamawa Emirate and returned to New York, where her exploits were deemed deserving of membership in the Order of Theseus." He cleared his throat. "I understand she is now living in the Order's headquarters, performing a variety of services there to earn her keep – as I said, she spent her entire fortune on her African expedition, and her family did not welcome her back. The exact reasons for this discord I do not know."

"Living at the Order? *Is* she?" I exclaimed. That explained why she had been the one to admit Betsy and myself, and perhaps why she had wanted to speak to us privately – she *needed* the money Aubrey Elliot's family had promised her, and probably would prefer not to share it.

That reminded me. "Can you tell me anything about Aubrey Elliot's sister?"

"Augusta Stallings? A very respectable woman; I understand her husband has made a fortune in shipping."

She existed, then, and her married name was indeed Stallings. Miss Darlington was sounding more trustworthy by the minute; if the Order had allowed her to live in their headquarters, her reputation among my fellow adventurers must be quite good.

I then allowed Dr. Pierce to turn me over to one of his subordinates as I set about learning all I could about Sebastien Boireau. I learned that his family fortune was founded by his great-grandfather, who had won something called the *Prix du galvanisme* in 1811. This award, created and presented by Napoleon Bonaparte himself, had carried a grand prize of 60,000 francs, and a medal valued at an additional 30,000 francs – more than enough, at the time, to make a man wealthy.

The odd thing was that this elder Monsieur Boireau's award was made in secret. The three earlier recipients of the *Prix du galvanisme* – or rather, half of it, since none of them had been deemed worthy of the full amount – had been announced publicly, with much fanfare, even though one of them was an Englishman and France had been at war with Britain at the time. But for the senior Monsieur Boireau there was no public mention of any kind, and the Archives had no mention of what the award was actually *for*. Apparently the Emperor had thought the full prize was deserved, but had considered Boireau's discoveries to be so dangerous that he had had them actively suppressed, and furthermore had discontinued the prize entirely, lest someone dig too deeply into its records and learn about whatever it was that had earned Monsieur Boireau his award.

This secrecy had served the family well; they had survived the fall of Napoleon unscathed, and they had continued to thrive under the restored monarchy, the Second Republic, and the Second Empire, making a good many well-placed investments in the latest scientific developments: photography, railroads, telegraphy, and so on.

None of this was of any immediate service in understanding the current Monsieur Boireau, or in devising stratagems for use against him, but I did not consider the time wasted. When I had concluded my research I thanked Dr. Pierce, and took my leave.

It was still too early to return to Hudson Street, so I decided to pay Tobias Arbuthnot's office a quick visit. Upon arrival I apologized for interrupting his day, but he assured me that he welcomed any distraction from certain unpleasant financial matters he was dealing with; in fact, what I had intended to be merely a brief greeting turned into a leisurely luncheon where we discussed everything *but* his business.

I had the distinct impression that there were ill winds blowing in the banking world, currents that seriously worried my friend, but I did not ask for details.

I did not tell him any details of my own recent activities, but I did let him know that should anyone question him about me, he was free to describe Mr. de la Rue's letter and anything I might have said about it. There was no need to maintain his usual discretion and respect for my privacy.

Naturally, he asked why, and I explained that while I did not yet feel free to disclose what I had learned, I expected that others might follow in my footsteps, and I did not want to block or discourage them.

By the time we finally parted ways it was late enough that I had to rush in a most undignified matter to reach Monsieur Boireau's Hudson Street office by 3:00.

Chapter Sixteen

Another Conversation with Monsieur Boireau

When I arrived at the Hudson Street office Monsieur Boireau's guard was still in place, but as soon as I reached the head of the stair he reached over and opened the door.

I stepped past and discovered that Monsieur Boireau was indeed present, behind the desk, as before. Nothing had visibly changed in the few days since our previous conversation. Mr. Cathcart once again occupied the chair by the window, while I took the same place as before. I set my hat on my knee as the other two guards left the room, closing the door behind them.

We exchanged quick greetings, and then Monsieur Boireau leaned back and said, "Now, Mr. Derringer, why did you wish to see me?"

"Well, sir, since last we spoke I have learned a few things. For one, I have learned that Professor Aloysius Vanderhart is in your employ and working in a private facility in New Jersey."

He frowned. "Oh?"

"I have been asked by his family to bring Professor Vanderhart safely home, and attempted to do so, but he was not permitted to leave the site. Letters he wrote to his wife in trust of your men have never arrived, and I'm afraid I must wonder whether they were ever actually mailed. A message assuring his wife of his safety was promised, but never delivered. I understand that you wish to keep your business private, but I must ask that you reconsider and allow Professor Vanderhart to visit his family."

He steepled his fingers. "And if I say I know nothing of this Professor Vanderhart?"

"It is not impossible that your Mr. de la Rue managed the entire matter without your knowledge," I answered.

"In that case, should you not have approached Mr. de la Rue, rather than myself?"

"I thought it better to deal with the man in charge, so that there could be no risk of misunderstanding."

He considered that silently for a moment, and I added, "Holding a man against his will is illegal, Monsieur Boireau, regardless of who ordered it. I have not yet spoken to law enforcement officers, but even if this was done without your direct instructions, I think the courts might well hold you responsible for the actions of your subordinates."

"And why have you *not* spoken to law enforcement officers, Mr. Derringer?"

"Because I would greatly prefer to settle this peacefully. I am not asking for any money nor an interruption in your research, Monsieur Boireau, merely that you allow the professor to visit his family, and that you allow him to depart freely when his contract runs out four months from now."

That I knew the terms of Professor Vanderhart's contract caused him to cock his head to one side and eye me warily. I suspect he was wondering what else I might know.

Boireau lowered his hands to the desktop. "I think you are confused, Mr. Derringer. I am not holding anyone prisoner. I do not know who this Professor Vanderhart is, nor where he might be."

I had hoped that he would be cooperative, but apparently that hope had been over optimistic. I had been playing my cards close to my chest, but I thought the time had come to show one. "He is in your walled compound on Wildwood Island, in Cape May County, New Jersey," I said.

Monsieur Boireau's frown deepened. "What nonsense is this?" His voice might have been very slightly unsteady – or perhaps that was my own imagination.

"I am told it is one of sixteen such facilities scattered about the globe."

"Why do you make these wild accusations, Mr. Derringer?" His voice rose in pitch. "Who are you working for?"

"I am working on behalf of the Vanderhart family. No, I am not in the employ of the secret masters of the Lost City of the Mirage. I know you believe they have agents everywhere, but I am not one of them."

Another card revealed. Monsieur Boireau suddenly straightened in his chair. Mr. Cathcart, I noticed, threw a look of surprise at his employer.

"Professor Vanderhart is studying the effects of pressure upon man–made structures, in case the Lost City should appear beneath the ocean," I added.

"Who have you told this nonsense?"

This was not going well. He was not willing to concede anything at all; my hopes for a civil and productive discussion and an amicable bargain were now very faint. Still, I was determined to keep trying.

I thought it might be significant that he asked who I had told, rather than who had told me. Still, I was concerned that if I kept going along this line he might realize I had visited the compound and spoken with Professor Vanderhart, so I suggested another possibility.

"You know, if you gather so many of the world's experts on electrical devices in one place, it should hardly surprise you if one of them invents a telegraph that does not require wires."

He appeared thunderstruck. "What? Who has done this?"

I ignored his question and continued, "I understand that you want to keep your business secret, Monsieur Boireau, and *I* want Professor Vanderhart's freedom. Can we not arrange an equitable exchange? I will give you my word that if the professor is home with his wife within the next three days, I shall say nothing of your plans to anyone – at least, anyone I have not *already* told and sworn to secrecy. Naturally, I have made sure that if I were to vanish, or perish, that everything I know of your activities will be spread far and wide – to adventurers seeking the scientists you employ, to law enforcement officers in every country where you operate one of your sixteen enclaves, and so on."

He pressed his lips together as he stared at me, then said, "Mr. Derringer, surely we can find an alternative."

That was the first time he had acknowledged that I possessed something he did not want revealed.

"Home with his wife and children within three days, Monsieur Boireau," I said.

"And how do I know you will not spread these...these stories on the *fourth* day?"

I cocked my head to the side. "Why would I want to do that? If you are correct, and the people of the Lost City pose a threat to our entire civilization, why would I want to disrupt the only effort to prepare a defense?" I shook my head. "All I want, Monsieur Boireau, is Professor Vanderhart's freedom."

"This is...is..." He looked at Cathcart.

"Blackmail," Cathcart supplied.

"*Oui, chantage*," Boireau said.

"And holding a man prisoner is kidnapping." I rose from my chair. "I do not think further discussion will be profitable, Monsieur Boireau. Take my word, I know more about your operation and your theories than I have said here today, but I will not reveal *any* of it to anyone I have not already told so long as Professor Vanderhart is safe at home on Sunday morning, three days from now, and I will ask the professor and those I *have* informed to remain quiet, as well."

"No, wait, Mr. Derringer! Who have you told?" Boireau also

stood; a moment later Cathcart did, as well.

"I am hardly going to reveal *that*, Monsieur Boireau!" I clapped my hat on my head and started for the door.

Mr. Cathcart stood motionless, apparently uncertain what was expected of him, but Monsieur Boireau came around the desk and headed toward me. I quickened my pace and opened the door.

"*Arrête-le!*" Boireau shouted. "Stop him!"

The guard who I had seen so often lounging just outside the door appeared in my path, hands raised as if to grab my arms. I decided not to allow that. I had trained in the martial arts, after all, though I had had little occasion to put those skills to use since I began my career as an adventurer. I delivered a solid uppercut to the man's chin, and he fell backward against the railing. For a moment I feared he might go over and crack his skull on the stair below, but he caught himself as I pushed past, and he grabbed at me as he straightened up. I pulled away before he could get a good hold.

"Three days, Monsieur Boireau!" I called as I trotted down the stairs.

The guard had not given up, though; he came trotting after me and tried to catch me by my shoulder in the building's entryway. Rather than resist I let him pull that shoulder back, but I whirled and brought my left fist around hard against the side of his head. He staggered, and another uppercut sent him sprawling onto the tile floor of the foyer.

His coat came open as he fell, and I noticed a Pinkerton badge on his vest. I did not linger for a closer look, but rushed outside and down to the sidewalk.

Boireau's other two guards had not heard any commands, but when they saw me dash out the door and across Hudson Street they exchanged glances, then came after me.

Fortunately, I had enough of a lead that I was able to dodge around a corner, then through an alley, and finally into a crowd where my pursuers reconsidered their situation and let me escape.

I proceeded a few more blocks with no particular destination in mind, merely a desire to put some distance between myself and Boireau's minions. I was pleased to have confirmation that at least some of his men were Pinkertons; at least I knew now that I definitely did not want to try hiring any of the company's men for myself.

It seemed unlikely, from the attitude he had displayed, that Monsieur Boireau would cooperate and release the professor, but I had given him three days, so I would not reveal anything until that time had passed. That did not mean, however, that I would do nothing. I turned my steps toward Perry Street and Snedeker's Tavern & Billiard Emporium, intent on warning Mad Bill of the situation.

The place was busier than during my previous visits, making it a little clearer how Mad Bill stayed in business; I realized I had never been there this late in the day before. Mad Bill was tending bar, while Mr. Dobbs waited tables. Neither noticed me immediately, but when I took a seat at the bar Mad Bill spotted me.

"Good to see you again, Tom!" he said. "What can I get you?"

"I'll have a beer, but mostly I came to speak to you, Uncle Bill."

He glanced at the crowd – which actually deserved the term "crowd," for once – and said, "I can't get away right now."

"It should only take a moment."

"Go ahead, then – what's happened?"

I quickly summarized the situation; we were interrupted briefly at one point by an order for a double whiskey, but were able to resume soon enough.

When I had finished, he said, "So little Sarah didn't realize who Uncle Bill is?"

"Apparently not."

He shook his head. "She'll probably figure it out soon enough. She's nobody's fool."

"You know her?"

"Oh, of course I know her! I've known her since she was a baby. But she and I had a bit of a falling out some years back, when I told her that her plan to go looking for her father was a bunch of damned foolish nonsense. She hasn't spoken to me since. I know I said she's not a fool, and mostly she isn't, but anything about her father is the exception."

"I understood that her mother and brothers advised against it, as well."

"They did, and she hasn't spoken to them since, either. I'm glad to hear the Order's taken her in; I was afraid she might be sleeping on the streets, or worse."

I nodded. "Has Betsy been here today?"

"Miss Vanderhart? She..." He stopped.

"She has," I said, as he frowned.

"She told me not tell you."

"Good. When you see her again, tell her what's happened."

"You seem very sure I *will* see her again."

I did not bother to reply to that. "I am going to disappear for a couple of days," I said. "You might consider changing your own habits, as well."

"I might," he agreed. "If I can. If I don't keep this damned place open, I don't make a living."

"Perhaps you could hire more staff? Perhaps Mr. Dobbs might know someone?"

"Maybe. We'll see. But meanwhile, Tom, you take care of yourself and don't worry about me."

"I'll do my best," I said, sliding off my stool. "Watch out for yourself, Uncle Bill." I picked my hat up from the bar and left.

My next stop was the flat on Eighteenth Street. I took a circuitous route, and circled the block to see whether I could spot anyone keeping an eye on the place. I could not, so I ventured in.

Betsy was not there, but she had left a note on the table, written in Kanta'an as we had agreed, assuring me that she was safe and well and was taking shelter elsewhere. As I had suggested, she did not say where.

I wrote my own note, in case she stopped back, struggling to remember the necessary vocabulary, and then left again.

That was Wednesday, April 23rd. I will not describe where I stayed or where I took my meals, in case I ever again need to stay out of sight for a time, but I took the opportunity to see some of the city's sights, such as the grand green vistas of Central Park and the glamorous shops of the Ladies' Mile. I did not see Betsy, nor Mad Bill, nor the inside of either the Pierce Archives or the Order of Theseus during that time. I did stop by the bank, not to see Tobias Arbuthnot, but to withdraw as much cash as I thought our family finances could afford; my operations had already proven rather expensive, and I did not want to have my actions limited by a lack of funds. I suspected that Toby might notice and inquire whether my mother knew what I was doing, but I did not let that worry me. I also decided I could risk sending Mrs. Vanderhart a telegram to reassure her that Betsy and I were well, and that her husband should be home again before too many more days had passed.

On Friday the 25th I arrived in New Brunswick and stopped in at police headquarters to speak to Detective Morris. I did not dare leave it until Saturday for fear he would not be at the station.

I knew that talking to Detective Morris might be a risk, since Betsy had suggested he might be in Monsieur Boireau's pay, but during my days of waiting I had had plenty of time to think, and I had concluded that was very unlikely. He had given me the key I needed to unlock the identity of the professor's abductor, after all, with that "day you'll rue" quote, and surely, had he been working for Boireau, he would not have done that. It would have been easy enough to simply not mention any specifics.

Fortunately, he was in his office. A sergeant directed me thither, and my knock elicited a call of, "Come in!"

When I opened the door he rose and held out his hand; we shook, and he directed me to a chair, then returned to his own seat behind his desk.

"Now, Mr. Derringer, what can I do for you? I will tell you at once that we have made little progress in our investigation of Professor Vanderhart's kidnapping. We have not yet located this mysterious Mr. de la Rue, though we can confirm that a man by that name was seen in New York City earlier this year."

"It seems I have been more successful than you, then – I found Mr. de la Rue and spoke to him, and I have met with his employer. I have been negotiating with him."

"Negotiating? I hope, Mr. Derringer, you have not agreed to pay a ransom!"

"No. I have made an arrangement, and if the kidnapper abides by it, Professor Vanderhart is to be freed and returned to his family by Sunday morning."

"Oh, really?"

"Those were the terms I gave him. I have little faith he will cooperate, however."

"I wonder that you did not simply ask me to arrange for his arrest."

"I considered it, I assure you, but I did not want to provoke an armed confrontation that might end in bloodshed. Further, I'm not certain just what authority might be needed. This man has a private estate well outside your jurisdiction, guarded by men I believe to be Pinkertons. I'm unsure whether he himself is a resident of New Jersey or New York State."

"Perhaps a Federal Marshal could take charge?"

"Perhaps. I had hoped to extract the professor without confrontation, though."

"I can't say I approve, sir. The law should handle these

things. Am I to take it you don't intend to identify the kidnapper for me?"

"Not yet."

"Then why are you here?"

"Because I fear I may have put the Vanderhart family in danger. The kidnapper may decide that it would suit him better to kidnap the rest of the family, rather than to release the professor."

He frowned.

"I would like to politely request that you have men posted to guard the Vanderhart residence, to ensure this does not happen."

"*I* would like to politely request that you tell me what the devil is going on!"

I sighed. "A millionaire has undertaken a massive research project, and rather than hiring scientists in the normal fashion, in order to keep his project secret he has abducted them and confined them to a laboratory complex. I have threatened to expose the entire scheme if he does not release Professor Vanderhart. I hope he will yield, but if he does not, I want to take measures to see that the Vanderharts are protected."

"But you won't tell me who it is, or where this secret laboratory is."

"Not until Professor Vanderhart is freed."

"And you aren't concerned about his other prisoners?"

"Of course I am! But I don't know which of his scientists are prisoners, and which are working for him voluntarily. I don't know what defenses he may have, or how he will react if the county sheriff, or a U.S. Marshal, arrives at his doorstep. The only leverage I have is my knowledge of things he does not want known."

"I am very tempted, Mr. Derringer, to have you arrested for obstruction of justice."

"I hope you will resist that temptation, Detective."

He glared at me for a moment, then said, "Get out of here,

Derringer, before I change my mind."

"And you'll send someone to guard the Vanderharts?"

"I'll see what I can do." He rose. "Goodbye, Mr. Derringer."

I rose as well, and left.

Chapter Seventeen

Breakfast with Miss Darlington

After leaving the police station I did not approach the Vanderhart family home directly, but observed it from a distance for some time. There were several suspicious individuals dawdling in the vicinity, but none I could identify with certainty as Boireau's men.

I was pleased to see a uniformed officer arrive around midday and take up a post under a shade tree across the street. I looked around for any sign that the policeman's presence had disturbed or discomfited anyone, but saw nothing at first.

Then I realized that most of the idlers I had noticed earlier had vanished. That worried me. I settled in to wait, fairly sure that the policeman had not noticed me.

Early in the afternoon I saw young Joe Vanderhart emerge and stroll up the street, apparently intent on visiting nearby shops. The policeman took note, glanced up and down the street, but stayed at his post.

I did not. I walked up the opposite side of the street and intercepted the boy as he stepped into a bakery.

He recognized me immediately, and exclaimed, "Mr. Derringer?"

I hushed him immediately, then pulled him aside and asked, "Has there been any word from your father?"

"No, sir, not yet."

"Your mother got my telegram?"

"Yes, sir."

"Have you heard from Betsy?"

"Only a telegram, sir. Same as you." Emboldened, he asked, "Why haven't you come to the house again?"

"I fear someone may be watching it."

"There's a copper across the street."

"I know. I meant someone else, someone more sinister."

He immediately looked around, as if expecting to see a cloaked figure lurking in the corner by the sweet rolls. I suppressed a smile.

"I may be worrying needlessly," I said. "Go on about your business. I have tried to arrange to have your father released and back home by Sunday morning. If your father *does* come home tonight or tomorrow, could you see that two lit candles are set side by side in the front window, as a signal to me?"

He nodded vigorously.

"And tell your mother not to be concerned; even if the professor is not released by Sunday, that simply means that my first approach has failed. I have several more to try." This was, I regret to say, an exaggeration. "However, I do not know what your father's captors are planning. I think it might be wise for you and your mother and siblings to be on your guard. Don't hesitate to speak to the officer if anything seems strange – he's there to protect you."

Joe nodded.

"And if you do see anything threatening, or if the officer leaves, you might all want to find another place to stay for a time. A friend's place, or perhaps with a relative?"

"I'll tell Mother."

"Good lad! Then I'll leave you to it." With that, I walked out of the bakery and strolled down the block.

The officer retired not long after nightfall, but I continued my own vigil, still hoping that Monsieur Boireau would see sense. Alas, no candles appeared that night.

Saturday was the same. A policeman stood guard across the

street, but there was no sign of the professor, and once full night had fallen the officer departed. I stayed on.

Perhaps an hour after midnight it began to rain, and I decided there was no need to linger any longer. As I began walking, I reviewed my situation.

Although it was still possible that Professor Vanderhart would turn up on Sunday morning, it seemed very unlikely; given the rail schedules he would have had to have left the compound by now, and I would have expected him to find some way to get word to his family. No messengers had arrived, so no such word had come. I thought I had no choice but to conclude that my first plan had failed. I needed to try another.

Revealing Monsieur Boireau's secrets was the obvious next step – I had made a threat, and failing to carry through on it would not be good for my reputation. Doing so, though, would not actually accomplish anything useful, so I saw no need to rush into it.

I did not see any other way to convince Monsieur Boireau to release the professor. I had made the most dire threat I could think of, without result. Blackmail had failed. Bribery – what could I offer a person who could afford to create his own international empire dedicated to electrical research? Appealing to his better nature seemed so absurd that I dismissed it immediately; he had made plain by his actions that he did not consider himself subject to ordinary moral restraints. I thought he probably sincerely believed that he was saving humanity, and that this end justified any means at all.

If Boireau would not release Professor Vanderhart, then someone else must. I could free him myself, I was certain, but was that the best option?

If I could find a way to convince his own employees to turn on Monsieur Boireau, that would be a better option than simply breaking in and bringing the professor out; in such an event Boireau would have more immediate and urgent concerns than recapturing the professor or retaliating against me.

If someone else were to break him out, without my direct involvement, then Boireau would have no reason to come after *me.* Whether he made an effort to recapture Professor Vanderhart would depend on the circumstances. Bringing in federal marshals – well, if the marshals actually managed to shut down the enclave on Wildwood Island, that would be an excellent solution, but is that what would happen? Monsieur Boireau was a wealthy man – a foreigner, but undoubtedly influential all the same – and he had Pinkertons in his employ; a confrontation with the marshals could easily turn into a bloody shootout.

At that, a confrontation assumed that the marshals were unified in opposition to Monsieur Boireau. I had read news reports on the Lincoln County War, out in the New Mexico territory, and deputy marshals had apparently fought on both sides there. Could I be sure none here would take Boireau's side? I would like to think that representatives of the federal government would be united in enforcing the law, but I could not be certain.

But there was another possibility, one that was actually more obvious and which might already be in process – what if a party of adventurers were to move against the Wildwood installation *en masse?*

This would be complicated by the fact that Monsieur Boireau definitely had adventurers in his employ, but there were plenty of others who were not, and who would be very interested in rescuing kidnapped scientists.

I therefore turned my steps toward the railroad station, leaving it to the New Brunswick Police Department to keep the Vanderhart family safe, with the intention of taking the morning's first northbound train back to New York City. I was determined to talk to Sarah Darlington, and if she had not already located Boireau's compound, perhaps give her a few more hints.

In the event, when I arrived at the headquarters of the Order of Theseus she was already on duty at the entrance. We went to breakfast together at a nearby restaurant.

After we ordered, I asked, "Have you found him yet?"

"Who? Your mysterious Frenchman, or Aubrey Elliot?"

"Either one."

"In fact, I believe I have found your so-called Frenchman, though he is actually a Belgian." She looked rather smug.

"Oh, you mean Leopold de la Rue? He's not the man in charge, merely a faithful lieutenant."

Her smile vanished. "Damn you, Derringer! Are you sure?"

"Quite sure. He works for a man named Sebastien Boireau."

She glowered furiously at me.

"Honestly, Miss Darlington, I congratulate you on getting as far as you have," I said, hoping to appease her. "I had an unfair advantage, in that Mr. de la Rue approached me to request that I speak to his employer."

"A fact you did not see fit to mention when last we spoke." Her rage did seem to be fading.

"That's right."

"But you're telling me now; what has changed, Mr. Derringer?"

"Monsieur Boireau has proven unwilling to release Professor Vanderhart peacefully."

"You spoke of the Frenchman's 'compound,' to use your word. Would that be the installation near Cape May that Mr. de la Rue visits every Wednesday?"

"Ah, you *have* found it, or at least gotten close! And yes, it is the site of these weekly visits you mention. Have you learned their purpose?"

"What would that be? Now that we are sharing information, perhaps you would enlighten me."

"Gladly, Miss Darlington. Wednesday is when all of

Boireau's employees on Wildwood Island are paid. Mr. de la Rue's weekly visit is to deliver the payroll."

She looked thoughtful, and just then the waiter delivered our plates.

A moment later, when the waiter had been thanked and had gone on about his business, Miss Darlington said, "Wildwood Island?"

"Oh, had you not yet located it exactly? Yes, it's on Wildwood Island, just north of Cape May. It's near an inlet on the northwestern side of the island. That's where Boireau is holding Professor Vanderhart and several other scientists, though he treats them as employees, rather than prisoners, and some may well be there voluntarily. There are also a good many workers who live in a village a little to the south of the compound, and they are all, scientists and staff, paid in cash every Wednesday."

"That would make sense. From the reports I have received, de la Rue always travels with guards on these weekly expeditions and always brings at least one large valise. I myself had seen him depart New York this past Wednesday morning and learned of his destination from the ticket agent. Then I sent a telegram to an acquaintance in Cape May to watch de la Rue and see where he went from the station. Unfortunately, my friend lost sight of him just north of town. I had intended to be in Cape May waiting for the train next Wednesday, the thirtieth, and see if I could do a better job of tracking him."

"Well, I may have saved you the trouble. I have no doubt that the enclave on Wildwood Island was his goal."

She took a bite of toast spread with pear butter, then said, "Why do I suspect, Mr. Derringer, that you are not telling me this simply from the goodness of your heart?"

"Because you aren't a fool. Of course I have a reason. Professor Vanderhart is in that compound, and I want to get him out safely. If you defeat Boireau and de la Rue and throw open the gates, then I can collect the professor and take him home to his family."

"And why did you not tell me this before?"

"Because I had hoped I could convince Monsieur Boireau to release him voluntarily, rather than risk a fight that might result in bloodshed."

"And Monsieur Boireau has not cooperated?"

"He has not."

She considered that as she ate a bite of boiled egg. "Surely, you could have found another way to free your friend."

"I could, and I may yet attempt it, but... Well, I foresaw complications."

"And you think I won't encounter these same complications?"

I shrugged, then caught myself; it seemed a somewhat rude gesture to make when dining with a lady, even if only for breakfast. "I don't know," I said. "I don't know what methods you might use to see if Mr. Elliot is there, or how you would go about extracting him."

"As I have not yet seen this supposed compound on Wildwood Island, neither do I," she said. "What more can you tell me about it?"

I proceeded to describe it as best I could, drawing some quick sketches in my pocket notebook to help with the details. I explained that the entire operation was intended to analyze the electrical devices of the Lost City and develop electrical weapons, though I did not say why Boireau wanted to do this. I described what I had seen of the compound's meager defenses and concluded, "I know that Monsieur Boireau employs some Pinkertons; I do not know whether they provide *all* of his guards, or merely a portion."

"Then *we* can't hire them."

"That was my conclusion, as well."

"Still, I think we can assemble a formidable team," Miss

Darlington said. "I have been speaking with our fellow adventurers and putting together an alliance."

"I trust you have been careful – I know Monsieur Boireau has adventurers in his employ."

"You and Miss Vanderhart did warn me of that, and I have been as cautious as I knew how. I think I can trust my allies."

"You understand that the entire purpose of the compound is to develop electrical weapons, don't you? We have no idea what they may be capable of."

"As you yourself said just moments ago, I am not a fool, Mr. Derringer. If we cannot achieve our goal by stealth or subterfuge, I believe I have a way to bring overwhelming force to bear before attempting a direct assault."

"I sincerely hope a direct assault can be avoided; I do not want to see bloodshed."

For a moment we sat in silence as I finished my coffee; then Miss Darlington leaned forward and said, "May I ask you a question, Mr. Derringer?"

"Of course!"

"Why did *you* not assemble a team of adventurers to aid you? You seem pleased that *I* have, but why did you not do it yourself?"

I sighed. "Miss Darlington, while I know I have already built something of a reputation among our fellows, the truth is that I am, as yet, inexperienced at the adventuring trade, and most of my own exploits have taken place out west – Arizona, California, Mexico, Utah, and so on. Most of the adventurers I know are either dead, retired, missing, or thousands of miles away from here. I have only the most casual acquaintance with most of the members of the Order of Theseus, while *you* actually live in their headquarters. I have no idea who can be relied upon and who cannot. Even the men my mother hired to train me in the skills she thought I would need – well, some are purely theoreticians, rather than adventurers; others are retired from active participation; and some I would not trust. They might well be on Boireau's payroll. You do not share these limitations."

She nodded. "You really should get to know more of us."

"I agree completely, and I look forward to doing so. For now, though, I am not equipped to organize a group of adventurers to take on a mad millionaire's private fortress, and you are."

"Well, I *hope* I am. I have never before attempted anything of the sort."

"If you would allow it, I should very much like to stop by the Order's headquarters every so often – daily, perhaps? To keep up with the situation."

"I would have no objection. Is there perhaps somewhere I can reach you, should I have news?"

"I am afraid not. I am more or less in hiding at present. Monsieur Boireau knows that I know a great deal about his operation, and I fear that he may try to ensure my silence. I hope you will be careful to avoid drawing his attention before you are ready."

"I will do my best, and thank you."

The waiter had brought the bill, and I settled that. Then I rose. "May I walk you home, Miss Darlington?"

"It would be a pleasure, Mr. Derringer." She took my arm, and we left the restaurant.

Chapter Eighteen

Another Visit to the Professor

The professor did not come home that Sunday, and I settled in for a prolonged effort.

I had taken a room at a boarding house in Brooklyn, but walked every morning across the magnificent new bridge, long under construction and finally completed just eleven months before, that connected that city to New York. I checked in occasionally at the flat on Eighteenth Street, at the Order of Theseus, and at Snedeker's Tavern & Billiard Emporium.

Mad Bill had taken three days off work, but then returned. Sarah Darlington had identified him as my Uncle Bill and had spoken with him, but neither of us thought any harm would come of that.

Betsy informed me, by a note at the flat, that she was alive and well, and staying with an old friend; she did not tell me where, but provided me with a few places I could leave a message for her, in case the flat was being watched. Her mother and siblings had gone to stay with friends – again, I was not told where – and I was assured that Betsy was able to reach them should the need arise.

Miss Darlington's own plans were proceeding. As she had told me, she intended to try stealth and subterfuge before resorting to anything direct. On Tuesday, April 29th, she made a trip to New Jersey, rented a boat, and steamed down the coast to Wildwood to scout out the terrain.

I only heard about this after the fact and expressed some

dismay that she had done anything so bold, but she assured me that she had not been spotted by anyone in the compound. She congratulated me on the accuracy of the description I had given her, but declined to tell me just what she had done while there.

I debated with myself whether I should investigate Wildwood again myself, rather than relying on Miss Darlington, and concluded that I should. Accordingly, following Miss Darlington's example, on a day when the weather was pleasant and seemed likely to remain that way, I hired a steamer to take me down the coast from Brooklyn – quite aside from sparing myself the inconveniences of trains and ferries, she was a larger boat than the *Eliza Anne*, not subject to the vagaries of the wind, and equipped with a dinghy. We set out from Red Hook and wound our way through the crowds of shipping, through the Verrazano Narrows and across the Lower Bay, then along the New Jersey shoreline.

I had assembled a few supplies, including a longer rope, in a canvas sack, and late that afternoon, when we were off the beaches of Wildwood Island, I had the dinghy lowered, dropped my bundle into it, and rowed myself ashore. The air was still unseasonably cool, but the work of pulling the oars kept me warm.

My crew had instructions to return every hour and watch for my prearranged signal – an oar stood upright in the sands of the beach by day, and a flare by night.

When I had grounded myself I climbed out and pulled my boat ashore, concealing it in a patch of brush just beyond the dunes. By this time the sun was setting; I slung the canvas bundle on my shoulder and headed for the enclave.

Uncomfortably aware that my father's journals often cited the dangers of repeating an approach to a hostile location, I moved forward cautiously, looking in every direction for sentries. Since I did not think Monsieur Boireau knew I had, in fact, visited the place, I was optimistic that there would be no new defenses, and in fact I did not see any. Perhaps he had accepted my impromptu suggestion that I had received my news by wireless telegraphy.

When I reached the wall of the scientists' compound I paused and retrieved a few items from my pack. Inspired by stories I had read I had brought certain supplies, and I readied them for use – I soaked a handkerchief in chloroform and sealed it into a cigarette case, which I slid into my jacket pocket. Thus equipped, I scaled the wall in the same location as before without any great difficulty – in fact, since I had come prepared, and equipped with a grappling hook, it was much easier than my previous attempt. I chose that location because I knew what lay on the other side of the wall at that spot; I did not want to risk arriving somewhere more visible.

Once again, I found myself in the little storage yard; I hid most of my supplies, then made my way to Professor Vanderhart's rooms, ignoring the whirring machinery, showers of sparks, and occasional flashes of artificial lightning.

I was, in my turn, largely ignored by those I encountered in the narrow streets. I had dressed to blend in, and no one paid any attention to me.

I headed for the professor's door, and along the way I had the unpleasant thought that they might have moved him to a different location, now that they knew someone in the outside world was interested in him. I wished that possibility had occurred to me sooner, and I was severely displeased with myself that it had not.

Well, if they had indeed relocated him, I would need to track him down. The compound was not exactly a vast metropolis; I should be able to find him in time.

But then I came to the passage where he had lived and concluded that they had not taken him elsewhere. I did not see him, but there was a guard in the same uniform as those at the gate posted by his door. The passage was otherwise deserted, which was fortunate.

Having started in that direction, I could not stop without arousing the guard's suspicions. I could have turned aside, I suppose, or simply walked past, but I preferred not to delay the inevitable; I marched up to the guard, then beckoned to him.

"De la Rue wants to see you at the gate," I said.

He looked at me with a puzzled frown, not moving from his post. "What?"

"Mr. de la Rue," I said. "He wants to see you."

"What the devil for?"

"How should I know? He just told me to fetch you."

The guard glanced at the professor's door. "And leave Vanderhart unguarded?"

"I can stand in for you until you get back."

He looked me over. "And who are you? I don't recognize you, and you're not in uniform. Let's see your badge." He reached under his coat and produced a revolver.

The man was not as stupid as I had hoped. Fortunately, I had prepared for several possible contingencies. "I've got it here," I said, reaching into the inside breast pocket of my own coat.

It was not a badge I pulled out, however, nor was it my own revolver; it was the cigarette case I had prepared moments before. I opened the case, pulled out the cloth, and lunged for his face.

He dodged, and brought his gun up, pointing it directly at my nose. I ducked, diving to my left, and threw a hard blow at his belly. He staggered, and I knocked his gun away with one hand while I clapped the chloroformed cloth on his face with the other.

He went down, with me on top of him, and struggled while I held the cloth in place.

Chloroform does not take effect as quickly as the dime novels would have you believe; it seemed to take forever before he finally stopped resisting, but at last he lay still, and I was able to roll off him and look around.

No one seemed to have noticed our little dispute. The various electrical devices that lined the street had apparently hidden us from the few people in the area, and the constant humming and crackling had hidden the sound of our struggle.

I dragged the unconscious guard around a corner and pushed him out of sight behind a tangle of glass rods and copper wires. I took his gun and explored under his coat, where I found a blackjack and a Pinkerton badge, both of which I appropriated and tucked out of sight in my own jacket. Then I brushed myself off, picked up my hat, and knocked on the professor's door.

I heard that familiar voice call, "Just a moment." I waited, and after a few seconds the door swung open.

"Mr. Derringer!" he exclaimed, upon catching sight of me. He looked around to see who else might be there, and when he saw I was alone he said, "Come in!" As I obliged him, he leaned past me and looked up and down the street. Then he drew back inside and closed the door.

"Wasn't there a guard?" he asked. "They started posting one here a few days ago."

"There was. He's asleep, just around the corner."

"Oh. Well, over here, then."

The place was much as I remembered it. The professor led me through the laboratory and its labyrinth of pipes into his sitting room, where we settled on the same velvet chairs we had used before.

"What are you doing here, Mr. Derringer?"

"Call me Tom," I replied. "I'm here to see just what your situation is."

"Are you going to get me out and take me home?"

"If you want me to, I can," I said, "but in truth, I had intended to wait a few more days. I expect a group of adventurers to carry out some scheme to disrupt this place, and I had thought that even if it does not succeed in freeing all the prisoners, it would provide a distraction so that you could leave unnoticed."

"But why wait?"

"Because, sir, Monsieur Boireau has made it plain he does not intend to let you go free if he can prevent it. I'm sure that's why a guard was posted – I attempted to negotiate your release, and this was Monsieur Boireau's response. Your family has gone into hiding, and I do not think it will be safe for *any* of you to return home until his entire enterprise has been brought down." I went on to describe what I had done and observed since last we spoke. "Now, I *can* get you out of here and off the island, but your absence would be noticed in short order, and I am fairly certain that Boireau's men would come looking for you, and your wife, and your children. If we wait a few more days, though, I expect Miss Darlington and her allies to confound Boireau's schemes sufficiently to render your escape beneath his notice. You therefore have a choice – leave now and put yourself and your family in danger, or wait here in comfort for perhaps another week and walk out untroubled."

"You're certain this Darlington woman can defeat Boireau?"

I hesitated.

"No," I admitted, "I wouldn't say that. I don't know her plans, her methods, or her capabilities. But I think she will provide enough of a distraction that your own departure will not be high on Boireau's list of problems."

"And if I choose to leave now, how would we do that? I cannot climb that wall, nor swim to the mainland."

"I have an axe," I explained. "I will chop a hole in the wall, and we will make our way down to the beach, where I have a small rowboat hidden. Then we will row out to sea, where I have arranged for a steamer to pick us up."

"Chop a hole? Won't that take some time?"

"Yes, it will."

"And won't it be noisy? What if someone hears and comes

to investigate?"

"Then I shall be forced to subdue him, as I did your guard."

"My guard? You said he was asleep!"

"He is. I chloroformed him."

"You *what?*"

"I dosed him with chloroform. Surely, you've heard of such things?"

"I've *heard* of them, but...you could have killed him! Chloroform is tricky stuff!"

"Well, let us hope I did not," I said, though I was shaken by his words. I had not realized that my actions were as dangerous as all that; after all, had Queen Victoria not used it in childbirth?

"Unless you left your poisoned cloth over his face, he won't be unconscious for long."

"Then we need to finish up here. Do you want to escape now, or wait?"

"He could be awake by now and waiting outside the door!"

As if on cue, someone knocked on his front door. I promptly hurried to hide behind the bed, and whispered, "Answer it!"

"I'll be right there!" the professor called. He rose, and walked out of my sight.

I could hear the conversation, though.

"You're here," the guard said, startled.

"Of course I am," the professor replied. "Where else would I be?"

"I thought...did you see a young man? Tall, athletic, wearing a brown coat and a bowler?"

"I haven't seen anyone. I've been working."

I could guess what was coming next, and I began crawling under the professor's bed. I resolved to never again use chloroform.

"You don't mind if I take a look around?" the guard asked.

"I don't suppose I really have any say in the matter, do I?"

I heard footsteps, and held my breath.

The man did not search the place exhaustively; he looked around, checked behind the bed where I had initially hidden, then turned and left the room.

"If you *do* see him," the guard said, "tell me or one of the other guards at once."

"Of course."

"Sorry to have troubled you, sir; I'll let you get back to work." Then his footsteps retreated, and I heard the front door open and close.

I immediately slid back out, got to my feet, and brushed myself off.

"I need to get out of here," I said, as the professor re-entered the room. "They'll be back for a more thorough search, I'm sure."

"Why didn't he look more carefully in the first place, then?"

"Because I took his gun," I said. "He's unarmed. He probably realized that if he found me without catching me by surprise he'd be at a severe disadvantage. But now he'll go for help, and whoever he brings back here will almost certainly have both weapons and numbers on their side."

"Then go!"

"Is there another way out?"

"No. But if he's gone for help, you'll have a few moments."

I nodded. "You'll need to wait. But I'll be back."

"Hurry!"

"One more thing, though," I said, as I walked through the laboratory with Professor Vanderhart at my heel. "Do you know whether Aubrey Elliot is in this compound?"

"Oh, of course he is. Here." I turned to see him lean over and snatch a sheet of paper from the clutter on his table. "I've been keeping a list of names; I thought you might find it useful."

I accepted the paper and quickly folded it and tucked it into an inside pocket. "Thank you, Professor." Then I hesitated, stepped aside just before reaching the door, and said, "Could you take a look?"

"Of course." He squeezed past, opened the door, and looked out.

"No one in sight," he said. "Hurry!"

I pushed past, and hurried.

I remembered which way led to the gate, where I believed the guard headquarters to be, and turned the other, ducking around the first corner.

It took some doing to find my way back to the supply yard, but I managed it eventually. Full night had fallen while I was in the professor's rooms, but electric arcs, Edison lamps, and sprays of sparks provided more than enough light to reach the rope; I clambered up it hastily.

Once I was outside the wall, however, the night was very dark indeed. The crescent moon was high overhead, but largely obscured by drifting clouds.

I made my way back to the beach, but stumbled several times, and needed some time to locate my boat; one clump of brush looks much like another in the dark. When at last I had dragged it down to the water I climbed in and began rowing.

Only when I was out beyond the surf did I pause long enough light the flare I had brought to signal the steamer by night. I hoped they were near enough to see its glare and would not confuse it with the electrical displays from Monsieur Boireau's enclosure.

I checked my watch frequently; it took some forty minutes before I finally spotted the steamer's lights, and hailed them.

That gave me plenty of time to upbraid myself for my inept use of chloroform.

One of the things about the life of an adventurer that does not receive much emphasis in the popular accounts is how much time is consumed waiting for something to happen, or traveling from one place to another. I had spent much of the preceding few months sitting in hotel rooms or on railroad cars, and had filled most of that time by reading whatever came to hand. Yes, some of it was worthwhile material, such as history texts, books of famous speeches, the memoirs of great men, and so on, but a great deal was cheap popular entertainment – dime novels and the like. In those stories chloroform is widely used, and an exposure of just a few seconds is shown to render the victim unconscious for hours with no significant after effects.

I had just learned that this was not, in fact, how chloroform works.

I had sometimes wondered why none of the tutors my mother had engaged to teach me the arts and skills of the adventurer's trade had ever mentioned using chloroform to deal with inconvenient guards; now I knew. I wished one of them had thought to warn me against it.

I wished also that Betsy had been present when I was making my plans and preparations; even if she was not intimately familiar with the chemical properties of chloroform, she would have thought to *ask* whether I knew what I was doing. I was *trying* to be more cautious and thoughtful in my adventuring, but obviously I still had some distance to go.

As I climbed aboard the steamer I wished Betsy was there, and not merely because of her good counsel.

Chapter Nineteen

The Gathering Storm

I was able to deliver the professor's list to Miss Darlington the following morning. Aubrey Elliot's name was indeed on it, and she took a great interest in several of the other names, as well. "I should be able to recruit another half–dozen adventurers with this," she said.

"And what will you do with them?"

"Quite possibly nothing. I'm still hoping for a subtler approach, but my attempts at bribery and subversion have failed, and I have not yet devised another method. I may resort to a direct assault, and in that case, the more men, the better."

I did my best to hide my shock and dismay at this; I did not like the sound of it at all. A direct assault? "Surely, you don't simply mean to charge in with guns blazing?" I asked.

"Not exactly. I have an approach I think will catch Monsieur Boireau and his minions off their guard. I have already made the necessary preparations."

I did not find this terribly reassuring. "And what would this be?"

"Oh, I don't think I want to tell you that, Mr. Derringer."

Her flippant manner did nothing to assuage my fears. "I had thought we had come to trust one another, Miss Darlington," I said, trying to match her insouciance, but I suspect my genuine dismay showed through.

"Not *that* much," she replied.

I forced a smile to hide my concern. I was beginning to regret giving Miss Darlington as much assistance as I had in locating Boireau's compound; she seemed distressingly untroubled by the prospect of serious violence. "As you please," I said. "Could you at least let me know when you intend to make your assault? I don't want to inadvertently interfere with it." In fact, if I could not prevent it entirely and avoid unnecessary bloodshed, I intended to capitalize on it. I certainly was not going to participate in any such ill-considered attack, nor did I have any interest in stumbling into the middle of a pitched battle, but if it proved unavoidable I could perhaps use it as a distraction while I rescued Professor Vanderhart.

"I don't mind telling you *that*. Since I have asked several people to assist me, I needed to let them know when their help would be needed; I couldn't very well expect them to be ready to go at any time. And a key element of my plans is not yet at hand. Still, if nothing changes, we will proceed this coming Wednesday, the seventh of May – probably late in the afternoon."

I had hoped that she had a more peaceful approach in mind; I had not come up with any brilliant stratagem, but she had more experience and resources I did not, so I had hoped she might devise something I could not. It was disappointing that she had, as yet, not done so.

I had also hoped that whatever resolution might be in the offing it might come a trifle sooner, rather than forcing the Vanderharts to remain scattered and in hiding for the next few days, but I did not say so. I had no clear notion of just how big an operation Miss Darlington had in mind; it might well be that she could not get the various pieces in place any sooner.

It was still good to have a definite date. I now knew I had those few days to try out any schemes of my own and to make my preparations.

I thanked her, and took my leave.

Now that I knew a little more of what might lie ahead, I would have liked another opportunity to speak with Professor

Vanderhart, but he was undoubtedly still under guard, and I now knew that chloroform was not an effective means for getting past his guardians. After some consideration I decided to attempt another approach regardless of the situation. I carefully reviewed what I had seen of his living quarters, and what I knew of his daily schedule; did he still take his meals in the dining pavilion?

For that matter, was the enclave as a whole still largely unguarded? My unfortunate adventure with chloroform must have alerted Monsieur Boireau's men that their walls were not sufficient to keep intruders out. His captors could no longer doubt that someone had penetrated their fortress

Further scouting was clearly in order, but the steamer I had rented previously was not available, nor could I find another on short notice, so on Friday, the second of May I took the train down to Cape May and booked a room at the Hotel Chalfonte once again. The following morning I chartered the *Eliza Anne*, assuring Albert that I would not ask him to sail up Post Creek again. Instead I had him sail up the Atlantic side of the island at a leisurely pace while I studied the shoreline with a fine pair of Porro binoculars I had acquired in New York two days before.

The weather was overcast and threatening, but as the entire spring had been unusually cold and wet I did not let that deter me in the slightest. With the glasses, there was enough light to make out activity on the island.

The workers' village was largely hidden by the island's natural brush, but I could see parts of it. I saw nothing remarkable there; a few women appeared to be going about their business, though circumstances did not allow me to make out the details. The wooden fortress was somewhat more visible, as it was larger and on higher ground, but the blank gray walls hid everything but the peaks of a few of the taller domes – or rather, everything except for a new addition to the structure.

There were men working at one corner, building what

appeared to be a sentry tower atop the wall. That was not a good sign. Perhaps Monsieur Boireau was abandoning the pretense that his scientists were employees, rather than prisoners. The framework was entirely inside the walls, of course – any exterior access would be too easily used by invaders.

I had Albert take me on up to the northeast end of the island, out of sight of the village and fortress, and I hoped of the unfinished sentry tower, and then bring me in close enough that I was able to wade ashore with my pack of tools and supplies. Then I took my time in walking back down to the enclosure.

I paused long enough to change my coat and to replace my wet trousers and boots with dry ones – though with the weather what it was, I doubted they would stay dry. I had brought along an outfit that I hoped would allow me to blend in with the workers, and I donned that. I circled around, keeping well clear of the crew working on the new tower.

So far there was only the one tower, but I glimpsed guards walking along the base of each wall. Entry was not going to be easy as before.

This was my own fault, of course; chloroforming a guard had made it obvious that someone unwelcome had been active inside the compound. My father's journals had always emphasized the need for the unexpected in dealing with a foe aware of your presence, and I was violating that rule by going back yet again, but I had not managed to devise a viable alternative.

Monsieur Boireau's men were probably not entirely sure whether the man who had chloroformed one of their number was an intruder, or someone who belonged inside but was now working against them, but anyone with any sense would take precautions against intruders. I hoped they had not yet determined how I had been able to get in and out.

I watched for some time, to assess just how many guards were patrolling outside the walls and how often they passed, and concluded that excluding the north side, where the gate was and where I dared not look, there were just three men, one on each side, marching back and forth – or at least, they were surely *meant* to be marching back and forth. In practice they did not so much "march" as "amble," with frequent pauses to lean against the wall and admire the sky or the sea, or to smoke a cigarette. Small canvas shelters had been rigged at each corner, and every so often two of them would meet under one of these and chat for a time. Clearly, if they had ever thought their duties to be urgent, that urgency had faded.

I had tried to prepare for every eventuality and slipping past guards had obviously been something I had considered, but I did not want to rush into anything. I hid myself in a clump of brush south of the fortress and took my time in studying the situation. Would the guards take a lunch break? Would there be a shift change? Either of those might provide the opportunity I needed.

And then a fat raindrop splashed on a leaf inches from my face, followed seconds later by another, and another...

Rain would decrease my visibility and make the guards more reluctant to venture out in the open. I smiled, and dug certain items from my pack.

The rain began to fall in earnest, and the guard on the near side of the fortress ran for the canvas shelter at the left-hand corner; a moment later he was joined there by his fellow from the western side of the enclosure, and the two of them huddled, staring out at the torrents Heaven had unleashed. I saw no sign of the eastern guard; presumably he had fled to the other end of his assigned route.

I needed to further distract the pair at the southwest corner, and I had come prepared; I raised the slingshot I had drawn from my pack, and fitted a good-sized stone in its pocket. I crept quickly to the west, until I had a good view of that wall, then took careful aim, drew the stone back to my shoulder, and let fly.

The missile soared over the canvas shelter and smacked

loudly into the wooden wall perhaps a hundred feet from the corner. Both guards heard it strike; I heard them speak, but could not make out the words. Then one raised a pistol and called, "Come on!" They both rushed out into the rain to investigate the source of the sound.

I had feared that they might be bright enough to leave one man on watch while the other sought the sound's origin, but fortunately they were not that well trained; both ran up the western side.

I promptly burst from concealment and ran along the southern wall, stuffing the slingshot in my pocket as I ran and raising the rope and grapple I had unpacked. The hooks caught on my first throw, and I scrambled up the wall as fast as I could, then hurriedly hauled the rope up behind me, and arranged it for the climb down into the enclosure. I was just testing it to be sure it was secure when one of the guards reappeared beneath the canvas, staring along the southern wall.

He did not, however, look up; perhaps the rain deterred him. At any rate, I saw no indication he had spotted me before I slid down into the fortress interior.

I was not in the same spot as on my previous two visits, but over a low building; I landed on the roof, doing my best to ensure that I did not make a loud thump. I then tried to figure out exactly where I was and how I might best reach Professor Vanderhart's rooms.

The roof where I crouched was bounded on one side by a tangle of wires and a metal framework, and whenever a raindrop struck the wires it would result in a brief flare of sparks and sizzling sound; another side faced a curve in one of the elevated tramways, though no vehicles were in sight, and a ladder on that side led down to a street. One side, of course, backed up to the sloping wall I had just crossed, and the last to a wall with a door in it, and an iron ladder leading to a higher level was bolted to the wall next to that door.

My initial notion was to descend to the street below the tramway, but then a thought struck me, and I reconsidered. Skulking through the streets until I could find a familiar area and make my way to the professor's front door was perhaps not my best option after all. I would undoubtedly be recognized as an intruder by any number of people.

If I climbed that other ladder, though, perhaps I could go from roof to roof until I found the professor's rooms. Oh, I might be spotted, but surely I would just be taken as a worker tending to some of the machinery. In an ordinary city traveling across rooftops would probably not be practical over any distance, but the buildings within the enclosure were jammed together and often connected by structures such as the tramways and other electrical apparatus I could climb across. If I ever did find myself in a dead end, it should not be too difficult to lower myself to the street.

With this in mind I began climbing.

The tops of Monsieur Boireau's collection of electrical laboratories formed a strange artificial landscape – domes and spires and towers connected by catwalks and rooftops, with sparking wires and metal rods scattered about. I could see the half–built watchtower in the far corner, but construction appeared to have been halted by the rain; I did not see another human being. There were moving gears and shafts visible here and there, various mysterious devices reared up toward the sky, and Edison bulbs cast their glow through the rain, but no one save myself had chosen to brave the elements.

It took me several minutes to orient myself; I located the storage yard where I had entered the enclosure previously, and then traced my route from there to the professor's rooms. Leaning over the edge of a neighboring structure I could see that there were now *two* guards posted at his front door, and I concluded that I could not reasonably expect to enter that way.

However, I was sure there were other ways in. One

possibility was to break through his laboratory ceiling – I could locate that precisely because several of the pipes from his experiments extended up through the roof into the open air – but I preferred not to do that much obvious damage. Instead I looked up the slope of the roof to the chimney that I had concluded connected to the fireplace in his bed–sitting room. I found seams between the brick and the surrounding roof where I could pry up the layers of tar paper and expose wooden sheeting. I had brought a saw, and it was simple enough to cut two of the planks, creating an opening large enough for me to lower myself into. That left me crouching on a joist in a narrow space between the roof and the room's ceiling; again, it was not difficult to cut the lath and break through the plaster below me. I kept as much as I could in one piece and set it aside.

I then carefully reassembled the planking and tar paper above me – I was sure it would leak, but I hoped it would not do such obvious damage as to render the professor's home uninhabitable, or to attract the attention of anyone else.

I was not surprised to find Professor Vanderhart waiting for me when I lowered myself and my pack down from the joist and dropped to the hearth; after all, my operations had been far from soundless.

"Good day, Mr. Derringer," he said.

"Tom," I reminded him, stepping down to the floor. "Good day, Professor. I hope you don't mind my means of ingress."

"Well, you have made something of a mess," he said, gesturing at the plaster dust and splinters of lath.

"I will be happy to clean it up, sir," I said, brushing myself off.

"And what brings you here today?"

"I thought it might be useful if we could exchange information. Our last meeting was cut short before I could ask many questions."

"Then you are not here with some damned fool idea about

lifting me out through that hole?"

"No, sir. I know better than that."

"Good. Then please, have a seat and ask your questions."

"We can talk while I clean up, surely?"

"If you prefer."

With that, I set to picking up the debris while I asked about his situation, what had happened since my previous visit, and what he could tell me of the other inhabitants of the compound. By the time I had wiped up as much plaster dust as I could and piled the bits of lath on the fire, we had moved on to more esoteric topics – what sort of electrical devices were being built and tested, and so on.

I also managed, somewhere in there, to explain that Sarah Darlington was planning an assault on the place on Wednesday afternoon, the exact nature of which I did not know, and that I would not be participating, but would instead cut a hole in the wall with an axe and fetch him out while the guards were distracted by the attack.

"I will have a boat waiting," I said, as I settled onto one of his fireside chairs. "No climbing or swimming will be necessary."

"You won't just wait until this Miss Darlington has defeated Boireau and his minions?"

"Honestly, I am not at all sure she and her allies *will* defeat them, and I am very much afraid that the attack will lead to fiery disaster, or at least significant bloodshed. After all, some of the electrical weapons you have described sound quite formidable."

"Well, if they work as intended they may be, but I have my doubts about just how my fellow scientists' theories will play out in practice."

"Nonetheless, sir, I am bound only to rescue *you*, and as I have serious doubts about Miss Darlington's scheme, I think my plan offers the best chance of success in that enterprise."

"Well, you may be right. It will be interesting to see." He glanced over at the hearth, then up at the ceiling. "The rain seems to be getting in."

"Yes, I see," I acknowledged. "But it's just a trickle."

That was, in fact, the case; water was running down the chimney to the hearth, but only a small stream, not enough to dowse the fire or run over the fender onto the floor.

"I'll clean it up," I said.

"You'll find mop, bucket, and absorbent rags in my workroom," he said. "I've had a few leaks in there, as well."

As I went to fetch the implements described, he called after me, "Will you be staying long?"

"I had not intended to."

"Then you won't stay until Miss Darlington's attack?"

"Oh, no; I have other matters to attend to, and as I said, I my plan calls for me to be outside the wall, breaking in to rescue you, with a boat just offshore, on Wednesday."

"Then could you take a message to my wife? Or my children?"

"Of course! I am not in so great a rush as that, and would be happy to do so." I did not mention that I did not actually know where the other members of his family *were* just then; there was no need to add to his concerns.

Chapter Twenty

An Unexpected Turn of Events

I stayed and chatted with the professor for most of the afternoon. I inquired as to whether he would be going to the dining pavilion and learned that his meals were now delivered to his door, to reduce his chances to communicate with outsiders; since there would not be enough for two in that delivery, I decided I should leave before suppertime to avoid any potential awkwardness.

Before my departure, though, I received answers to a great many questions. I learned that several of the other scientists had realized they were prisoners and were eager to leave, but they were not, as yet, a majority – most were more than satisfied with the money they received and were happy to trade their freedom for it, especially since they had no other way to finance their research.

Professor Vanderhart himself had been under guard ever since I had spoken to Monsieur Boireau demanding his freedom. He had been asked whether he wanted to leave, and when he replied that he did, that first guard had been stationed at his door. He had not been abused or threatened, though, merely told that he would not be allowed to go until the Lost City had appeared again.

I learned many details about just who the various scientists were, and what they were working on. A great many of their researches seemed to be ending in failure; so far as the professor knew, no one had yet managed to make a single device from the

Lost City function beyond emitting a faint glow. In fact, no one had yet determined what any one of them was intended to do. Many of Boireau's employees had, however, created their own electrical devices. The professor knew few details, but he had seen electrical discharges that looked like artificial lightning, machinery that performed any action a steam engine could accomplish, electromagnets that performed miracles of levitation, and much more.

My bluff about someone in the compound inventing a way to operate a telegraph without wires had resulted in a great deal of questioning, but no one had admitted to having created, or even considered, such a device. Several people had pointed out that lights or flags could be used to send messages without requiring any sort of exotic technology, but Mr. de la Rue and his minions had replied that those could easily be seen by others, while this mysterious new sort of telegraph would presumably be entirely private. It was rumored that scientists in some of Boireau's *other* compounds had been assigned to create exactly the sort of message system I had suggested.

The professor's own research had yielded very little; he had determined that it would absolutely be possible to build structures that could survive the pressure of the ocean depths, but whether the structures of the Lost City could, he could not say – he simply did not have enough information.

We discussed the possibility that Sarah Darlington, or some other adventurer, might find a way to extract the scientists peacefully. The professor assured me that if they were, in fact, released prior to Wednesday afternoon, he would do his best to inform me; I provided him with several possible places he might reach me by one method or another.

All in all, it was a very educational afternoon. I would have enjoyed it more if I had not had to mop up water from the hearth several times before the rain finally stopped. With that in mind, when at last I ascended a rope into the rafters I took with me some of the adhesives and tape that Professor Vanderhart had on hand for his experiments, and before leaving I did my very best to re-seal the opening I had made in the roof.

That done, I made my way back to the outer wall.

As I did, I saw that workmen were climbing the unfinished watchtower. At least two of them glanced over my way, but apparently did not see anything particularly suspicious about a young man carrying a pack across the roofs of the compound. I suppose they assumed I was a workman attending to some legitimate business, and of course I had chosen my attire with that in mind.

When I reached the wall, though, matters were not so simple. The guards were still down there, patrolling their various sides of the square. Fortunately, I knew a trick or two.

I made my way to the west side of the enclosure, well away from the corner, where I tied an extra rope around the beam inside the top of the wall; then I waited until the man walking the south wall appeared under the canvas at the corner to exchange a few words with his western counterpart.

I tossed a hammer into the bushes below, where it made a very satisfactory rustle and thump, drawing the attention of both guards; then I dropped my rope down the wooden slope of the wall.

"Look!" one of them shouted, and they both trotted toward the rope, guns drawn.

I, however, hurried as quickly as I dared back to the south wall – I could not run full out for fear of losing my balance, but I managed a good pace, crouched down so that I could not be seen by that pair. Once I was safely around the corner I secured a hook, dropped another rope, and slid down as quickly as I could without injuring my hands. Once on the ground I shook the hook free and gathered up the rope as I ran southeastward, toward the beach.

Once on the sands beyond the dunes I made my way south.

Perhaps a quarter-hour later I spotted the *Eliza Anne* off the shore, and signaled; Albert brought her in close enough that I could wade out perhaps halfway and swim the rest. The water was not discernibly warmer than on my first visit, and I was shivering miserably by the time I pulled myself aboard. Albert had thought to bring a good supply of towels. Before the last light had faded from the western sky we were sailing into the harbor at Cape May, and when we docked I was only slightly damp and chilled.

I stayed another night at the Chalfonte, and after breakfast I made inquiries as to whether anything out of the ordinary might have happened on Wildwood Island overnight; there were no such reports. I decided I had things I had better do back in the city – primarily messages to deliver. There were fewer trains on Sunday, but I was able to get back to New York before suppertime.

After taking a room at a cheap hotel – not the Robertson, nor anywhere else I might be recognized – I deposited my pack there, then ate at a little restaurant on Murray Street. After that I ventured to our next pre-arranged hiding space, behind the plaque on the Montgomery Monument at St. Paul's, where I found a note from Betsy, once again written in our version of Kanta'an. She assured me that she was well, let me know that she had made contact with her mother, and suggested a spot at City Hall where we might hide our next round of notes.

That was excellent news, and I wrote a reply, telling her that one way or another, her father should be free some time Wednesday evening; I suggested we might risk meeting at the flat on Eighteenth Street at 1:00 on Thursday afternoon, where I could restore him to the bosom of his family, or perhaps, if she preferred, we could meet at the Hotel Chalfonte in Cape May on Wednesday night. If I did not hear from her at the hotel, I would assume it was to be the former.

I secreted my message in the agreed–upon spot, and then set

out upon a little reconnaissance, stopping by Monsieur Boireau's office on Hudson Street, and then strolling around the headquarters of the Order of Theseus, though I made no attempt to go into either building. I did listen unobtrusively to people who were entering or leaving.

There were no signs of unusual activity at either establishment. In particular, there were no indications that Sarah Darlington had found an alternative to a direct attack on the compound. I debated trying to have a word or two with her, to make one last attempt to dissuade her from making her planned assault, but decided against it, as it might draw unwanted attention from anyone who saw us together.

Besides, at this point I had built much of my plan on using the attack as a distraction; I was not certain I still *wanted* to dissuade her. If I had some way to ensure that the attack would not trigger bloodshed nor cost any lives, then I *did* want it to take place on schedule; it was the utter absence of any such assurance that had me concerned. I did not want to be in any way responsible for a slaughter.

The evening was well advanced by the time I returned to my hotel and went to bed.

On Monday morning I wired my mother to let her know I was well, and that I hoped I might at last return home by the end of the week. I spent the rest of the day and all of Tuesday in performing various errands and in enjoying the spring weather that had finally arrived, at least temporarily. The sun had finally reclaimed the sky from the rain clouds that had dominated so much of the spring, so that I was able to sit comfortably in Union Square and read for much of Tuesday afternoon.

I checked our chosen message cache at City Hall on Tuesday, and found a note from Betsy saying she planned to meet me at Cape May on Wednesday night, but her mother and siblings would return to the family home in New Brunswick and wait for us there.

I had some doubts about the wisdom of returning to New Brunswick, but I dismissed them; I had no way to get any message to the Vanderharts in time to do any good, and they were probably safe enough there.

Then Wednesday morning arrived, and I arose bright and early and took my breakfast at a nearby café. I bought a copy of the *New-York Times* to read while I ate, but did not bother to glance at it until I had placed my order with the waitress.

When she had left, I picked up the paper and read the first story on the first page. "Wall Street Startled," the headline read. "Marine National Bank closes its doors."

I blinked. I knew that I had heard about the Marine National Bank recently, but it took me a moment to recall the context.

Then I remembered.

That was Monsieur Boireau's bank. He had paid his fees at the Pierce Archives with drafts drawn on that bank. Mr. de la Rue withdrew the weekly payroll for all Monsieur Boireau's employees on Wildwood Island from the Marine National Bank every Wednesday morning, then personally delivered it.

Except it appeared that he would not be doing so this week.

I read on, and learned that the bank had debts and obligations far beyond its ability to pay; someone by the name of Ferdinand Ward who sat on the bank's board, and James Fish, the bank's president, had apparently lost at least half a million dollars of the bank's money in unwise real estate speculation. Mr. Ward could not be found and was said to have fled the city, while Mr. Fish was said to be secluded in his office, trying to make sense of the situation.

In total, $700,000 had gone missing.

Ex-president Grant and his son were involved in the sorry affair through the brokerage firm of Grant & Ward, named for the younger Ulysses Grant and the aforementioned Ferdinand Ward; neither of the Grants appeared to have been directly involved in the mismanagement that led to the firm's collapse, but it was Grant & Ward's failure to pay the considerable sums owed that had forced the Marine National Bank to shut its doors.

The story mentioned, anecdotally, one fellow who had come to the bank that morning intent on withdrawing money, who, upon learning there was no money to be had, had gone around the corner to the office of one of the bank's directors and loudly threatened legal action, whereupon he was removed by force. I wondered if perhaps that had been Mr. de la Rue.

But no, that had been Tuesday morning, and Mr. de la Rue made his withdrawals on Wednesdays. Any pleasant fantasy I might have of his violent ejection from someone's office was merely that, a fantasy.

Still, I realized, this changed everything. So far as I knew, Sebastien Boireau's power came entirely from his wealth. He had no authority beyond what his money bought him. He was able to hold Professor Vanderhart captive because he paid the Pinkertons to do so. He had not used any sort of moral argument or rational persuasion to build his empire, but only his money. He had deliberately chosen to rely on his personal wealth to convince others to support him, rather than trying to sway them with explanations of the perceived threat from the Lost City of the Mirage. While perhaps understandable after having had his pleas rejected by various governments, this dependence on money was now shown to be a possible weakness. He undoubtedly still had the majority of his fortune safely tucked away somewhere in his native France, but by all indications he had kept all of his liquid assets on this side of the Atlantic at the Marine National Bank, where he and Mr. de la Rue could no longer get at them. There would be no payroll delivered today.

That might be just what I needed to prevent needless bloodshed.

I ate quickly, and then hurried out to the street, where I

flagged down a newsboy and bought his entire stack of the *Times*, some thirty copies. I considered looking for more, but decided that these would be sufficient, and I had a train to catch. I made a quick return to my room, where I packed my belongings; then to the desk to settle my bill, and I was on my way once more, back to Cape May.

Chapter Twenty-One

Miss Darlington's Scheme in Action

My train arrived at 2:30 in the afternoon. I returned to the Hotel Chalfonte one more time, where I made my final preparations; then I set out to engage the *Eliza Anne* again, for what I believed would be the last time. I had my prepared pack, with axe, ropes, gun, and all the usual tools – and with thirty copies of the *New-York Times* added.

I did not know the exact time of Miss Darlington's planned assault, nor its nature; I hoped that it had not already begun, and that I would be able to reach the fortress before she and her allies did. Perhaps news of the failure of Monsieur Boireau's bank could forestall the entire thing. I asked Albert to take me up the west side of the island again, to see just what was happening, and he agreed, with the understanding that I would not ask him to enter Post Creek.

We set out shortly before four, and with the help of a brisk west wind we quickly made it past Thoroughfare Island into Jarvis Sound. It was there that we first spotted the smoke.

"What's that?" I asked, pointing.

"Looks like a steamer," Albert replied.

"Here? Not out on the ocean? Isn't it a little shallow?"

Albert shrugged. "I would have thought so," he said.

The source of the smoke was moving northeastward, up the channel into Sunset Lake – our own intended course. We followed, and even gained ground on the mysterious steamer.

We came around Shaw Island without getting a good look at it, but then, as we rounded a headland, I finally had a clear view.

I stared, astonished, at the huge gray metal monstrosity chugging its way up the channel.

"That's a monitor!" I said.

It was, indeed, one of the famous warships, the first of which was notoriously described as "a cheesebox on a raft." The cylindrical turret stood high out of the water, but the deck was so low that the hull was almost invisible. A circular canvas awning shaded the turret, and I could see figures standing atop the turret beneath that awning. I did not see any guns; presumably they were pointed forward, on the far side from my own position.

What, I wondered, was a naval vessel doing here?

Then I realized that the boat was flying no ensign, and those figures on the turret were not in uniform. In fact, one had long white hair and wore a blue dress.

This was Sarah Darlington's secret weapon.

"Where the devil did she get a monitor?" I said aloud, speaking more to myself than anyone else.

"Who?" Albert asked.

"An adventurer I know," I replied. "I believe that's her in the blue dress." I pointed.

"You know, I saw all those pictures from the war, with the *Monitor* fighting the *Virginia*," Albert said. "I never realized how *big* the *Monitor* was."

He had a point; the simplicity of its design made it easy to underestimate the size of a monitor. While nowhere near the size of the largest modern battleships, it was not a small vessel. This one appeared to fill practically half the width of the channel.

I wondered whether anyone aboard the ship had yet noticed our own little craft. We had no smoke, no chugging engines, to draw their attention. The people on the turret all seemed to be looking to the east, toward Wildwood Island and the strange wooden fortress thereon. I looked that way myself and could make out one of the newly added watchtowers and the peaks of two or three domes.

"I think I'd like you to put me ashore soon," I said.

"Good," Albert said. "I don't think I want to get much closer to that machine."

"Up ahead," I said, pointing. "Where the channel narrows; the shore of the island looks pretty solid there."

Albert nodded. "The water's deep enough to get close in," he said. He shifted the tiller. Then we both looked ahead at the monitor again.

We both stared in amazement as it did not turn with the main passage, but instead steamed directly into Post Creek.

"They're mad!" Albert said. "They'll never get that thing in there! And if they do, they won't have room to turn it around to get back out!"

I was trying to think how to best word my agreement when there was a tremendous grinding sound and the ship ahead of us shivered violently, then stopped moving.

"You're right," I said. "They've run aground." I looked up at the bank above them. "They're in range of the compound, though."

"The what?"

"Never mind. Just get me ashore."

Albert shrugged. "Whatever you say." He steered the *Eliza Anne* to starboard   .

As I clambered ashore with my pack I could hear voices shouting aboard the monitor – and other voices shouting on the shore. I was not able to make out the words, but my impression was that the two sides were shouting ultimata back and forth. I hurried up the slope, pushing my way through the brush.

A moment later I emerged onto the cleared land around the compound, where a guard was pretending to patrol the western wall. In fact, he was clearly trying to listen to the dialogue between ship and shore, and paying little attention to anything else. I made no attempt to hide my approach, but he failed to notice me until I was perhaps a dozen yards away, waving at him. When he finally spotted me I called, "Hallo! I need to see Mr. de la Rue!"

He belatedly drew a revolver and pointed it at me; moving deliberately, I raised my hands. "I'm here with a message for Mr. de la Rue," I said. "Can you take me to him?"

"Is it about that monstrous metal ship?" he asked.

"More or less," I said.

He hesitated, then lowered his gun and beckoned. "Come on," he said.

He made me walk a couple of paces in front of him, his gun once again at the ready and aimed at my back, and directed me to and around the northwest corner, beneath the newly-built watchtower there.

As we marched from the corner along the northern wall I could see the top of the monitor's turret some distance away to my left, with half a dozen people standing on it, and ahead of us the enclosure's gate, with three men standing atop that. The turret had rotated so its two immense guns were aimed directly at the gate.

And at last I could make out some of the dialogue between the two. A man on the ship was bellowing through a megaphone, "...final warning! If you do not surrender within the next ten seconds, we will open fire!"

One of the three men atop the gate raised a megaphone of his own and shouted back, "Go to Hell!" Another was turned to face the compound and was making a great looping gesture with one arm, as if in imitation of a windmill.

"Ten!" the man with the megaphone aboard the monitor shouted. I thought I could see someone next to him holding out a large watch.

Something inside the enclosure hummed loudly, and a metal contraption unlike anything I had ever seen rose up from behind the wall. It had a narrow conical peak encircled by half a dozen brown rings perpendicular to the cone's axis.

"Nine!"

The cone continued to rise.

"Eight!"

The cone now stood atop a framework of metal beams that cleared the wall by several feet.

"Seven!"

I picked up my pace.

"Six!"

The cone began to pivot, pointing its tip toward the basin – and toward the ship therein.

"Five!"

I was trotting now; I glanced back over my shoulder and saw that my escort had stopped in his tracks, staring at the machine above the wall.

"Four!"

The machine turned, bringing the point of that cone to bear on the monitor's turret. One of the men on the gate had noticed me and was pointing me out to his companions. I waved.

"Three!"

The humming began to rise in pitch. I broke into a run, waving wildly.

"Two!"

The tip of the cone began to glow red, and sparks rained from it.

"One!"

Two of the three guards were now watching me, while the other kept his attention focused on the monitor.

"Zero!"

Simultaneously, the ship's guns roared, and the cone spewed out a bolt of lightning. The flash of the cannon was almost lost in the astonishing blazing brilliance of the artificial lightning, and the smoke that billowed up from the guns was lit vivid orange, like a storm cloud lit from within.

The lightning bolt struck the monitor's turret, but had no discernable effect beyond showers of sparks here and there; I knew enough to realize that it must have grounded out through the metal hull and the water beneath, as if the ship itself was a gigantic lightning rod. The figures on the turret jerked and staggered, but none of them fell; I guessed that some tiny portion of that immense burst of electricity had reached them, but not enough to do any real harm.

Meanwhile, the shells from the ship's guns tore through the upper edge of the flimsy wooden walls of the compound, still rising; as best I could judge, they would either pass entirely over the rest of the enclosure, or knock the tops off a couple of the domes. From somewhere behind the wall came a spray of sparks.

I reached the gate and shouted, "Stop! There's something you need to know!"

"Are you ready to surrender?" came a hail from the ship.

The man on the gate raised his megaphone, but I waved desperately and shouted, "Tell him you need to discuss it!"

He paused, and glanced down at me. "Who the devil are *you?*" he asked.

"Tom Derringer," I said. "I'm here to talk to Mr. de la Rue – it's vitally important!"

"De la Rue isn't here. Now..."

"*Shouldn't* he be?" I interrupted. "Isn't it payday?"

The man on the gate glanced at his companions.

"I know why he isn't," I called. "I know where your pay is."

"Did those bastards *steal* it?" He turned. "Harry, get the electromagnet ready."

"They didn't steal it! Let me show you!" I dropped my pack and pulled open the flap, groping for the bundle of newspapers.

Two other guards had emerged from the gate, and the man who had been watching the western wall came up behind me. "What are you talking about?" he asked.

I pulled out the papers. "Look, I'll show you! You aren't going to get paid, any of you! The money's gone!"

"Well?" came a call from the monitor.

"Hold on!" the man above the gate called back. "We're discussing it!" Then he looked down at me. "What's this about?"

I held up a copy of the *Times*. "Boireau's bank has gone bust!" I shouted. "He can't pay you! He can't pay *anyone!*"

"Give me that," one of the guards on my own level barked, snatching the paper from my hand. I pulled another from the stack and held it up so that one of the trio atop the gate could stoop down and reach it.

The three men on ground level were now sharing their copy, reading the featured story. The three above the gate also held theirs in common, reading it.

"The Marine National Bank," one of them said. "That's what it says on the purses every week."

"It's where Boireau had *all his money!*" I cried. "De la Rue isn't here because he can't get the money to pay you!" I gestured in the direction of the warship. "Do you want to see this place get knocked down around your ears and not even get *paid* for it?"

"Go get Andrews," the man with the megaphone ordered, and one of his companions hurried through a door into the compound.

"What's going on over there?" demanded Miss Darlington's spokesman. "We've got the range now; our next shot will take down that infernal machine of yours!"

The enclosure's spokesman looked up at the lightning generator. "Harry, shut that thing down," he said. "It didn't do a damn bit of good against the ironclad anyway."

"What about the electromagnet?"

"Keep it ready." Then he knelt down and beckoned to me. "Give me those newspapers."

I handed him perhaps half my supply. For a moment he seemed inclined to argue and demand the rest, but then he shrugged and stood up, just as a man in a business suit appeared from inside the compound.

"What's going on?" the newcomer demanded.

He and the spokesman huddled together, speaking quietly; the spokesman held out a copy of the newspaper.

One of the ground-level guards took a newspaper and vanished through the gate.

I waited patiently, handing out another half-dozen copies of the *Times* as men came and went, talking among themselves.

After a few moments, the man on the ship called, "What's going on over there?" A grinding noise came from the lightning generator, and it began to sink back down out of sight.

Finally, the man atop the gate lifted his megaphone again and called, "What are your terms?"

There was a pause, and I could see the people on the ship's turret conferring. Finally, the spokesman's voice boomed out again.

"You must release all the scientists and other prisoners! We will transport them back to the mainland and arrange for them to return home to their families."

"What if they don't want to go?"

That seemed to baffle the crew of the ironclad. While they were arguing, the man on the gate raised his microphone again.

"Listen," he said, "we're done here. You can come and do whatever you like." Then he dropped the megaphone, turned, and walked through the door into the compound.

Unsure what I should do, I stood waiting, handing out copies of the *Times* to anyone who wanted one. Men came and went through the gate for several minutes; then the gates opened wide and men began to stream out. Where up until now everyone I had seen on the shore, save the one man in a business suit, had been guards, in their standard uniform, now I saw people in a variety of clothing, including white coats, emerging. Most of them were heading down to the little pier – but the steamer wasn't there. Presumably it was in Cape May, waiting for Mr. de la Rue.

And looking at the basin and the upper end of Post Creek, I didn't think it would fit past the ironclad.

The people atop the turret seemed to have finished their argument; a man raised the megaphone and called, "We'll send a boat!"

I looked at the crowd gathering on the dock. "You'll need more than one," I called, to no one in particular.

Then I pushed past the exodus and through the gate, making my way into the enclosure to find Professor Vanderhart.

Chapter Twenty-Two

Professor Vanderhart's Homecoming

I will not bore you with the details of the evacuation of Wildwood Island. The operation was haphazard and disorganized, and it was not until midday on Thursday, the eighth of May, that everyone who wanted to leave had left.

Miss Darlington's monitor had to unload most of its crew and supplies and wait for the tide to rise, before it could be freed from the mud of Post Creek; in fact, it required a tug from a gigantic electromagnet in Monsieur Boireau's fortress to jar it loose. Once freed, however, the crew wasted no time in taking aboard roughly a hundred of the island's erstwhile inhabitants.

Professor Vanderhart and I did not wait, however; once I had found the professor we gathered up his luggage, including a valise that held his accumulated pay, and made our way to the shore, where I signaled Albert as agreed. The professor, half a dozen of his friends who had seen where we were going and followed along, and I all waded out into the cold water and boarded the *Eliza Anne* without mishap and made it safely back to Cape May in time for a late supper. I suggested to Albert that he might find paying passengers if he were to make a return trip, and I believe he acted upon this suggestion, as he was already putting out to sea once more by the time we were out of sight of the dock.

I led the way back to the Hotel Chalfonte, where the professor and I were both delighted to find Betsy seated in the lobby, a book in hand. She caught sight of us at the same instant I spotted her; she dropped her book and leapt up from her chair with a shriek of joy. "Papa! Tom!" She ran toward us, and I stepped back, to make sure that her father received the first embrace.

When at last she and her father released one another Betsy turned and gave me a more restrained embrace. When we stepped apart she said, "Thank you, Tom." She looked at her father, and I saw tears in her eyes.

I could not find suitable words, and simply nodded.

We then turned our attention to more practical matters; Betsy and her father booked two more rooms on the same corridor as my own, and after depositing our rather scattered collection of luggage we gathered for supper in the hotel's restaurant.

It was a very pleasant meal, though we were all tired from our adventures. The food was good and we had a great deal to tell one another. Betsy and I exchanged a few remarks in Kanta'an, to the professor's bafflement. We proceeded to tell him everything that had happened since we headed West the previous year – our first encounter with Teddy Hancock aboard a westbound train, our explorations in San Francisco, our adventures in, around, and under Los Angeles, our return to San Francisco and our meetings with the nameless committee there, and our adventures in the Wasatch Mountains of the Utah Territory.

He, in turn, told us about his exploits in the South Seas, and what he had seen of the spectacular devastation left in the wake of Krakatoa's destruction.

That was followed by an exchange of accounts of our various meetings with Mr. de la Rue and Monsieur Boireau and their minions, and how I had located the encampment on Wildwood Island. I explained how we had met Sarah Darlington and how she had followed my hints in her own mission to find and free Aubrey Elliot.

By this time our plates had been cleared away, and we were

well into our second round of coffee, when the professor asked, "Tom, where did Miss Darlington get a *warship?*"

"I have no idea," I admitted. "It's as great a mystery to me as to you."

Someone overheard that exchange, and the next thing I knew half a dozen of the other newly freed scientists had joined our conversation. We learned of the difficulties encountered in refloating the ironclad, and that those who chose to ride it had been crammed on the deck, not allowed below. Their journey back to Cape May had not been particularly comfortable, and they had not yet had time to eat their supper, but they were free and safe.

Not everyone had trusted the monitor – understandably, I thought, given how low it rode in the water and that it had already run aground once – so many people had still been on the island at last report. In fact, some, I was informed, intended to stay on – they did not care to abandon their research even if they were no longer being paid.

The hotel's serving staff had begun to show the faintest polite signs of impatience, so we left the restaurant and moved our conversation elsewhere. Late that evening, as we were relaxing in the lobby of the hotel, I was surprised to see Mr. Leopold de la Rue walk in, in the same European coat and Homburg hat he had worn when I first saw him in Philadelphia but looking somewhat the worse for wear.

I stood, unsure whether to expect either a verbal or physical attack. Professor Vanderhart tensed in his chair, and Betsy reached a hand toward her bosom, where I knew she sometimes concealed a small pistol.

Seeing me, de la Rue stopped. He made no hostile movements; instead he briefly doffed his hat. "Mr. Derringer," he said. "I thought I might find you here."

"Mr. de la Rue," I said, nodding. "I did *not* expect to see you. I believe you missed your usual train today, and I was unaware you had caught a later one."

"I did miss my customary train, yes," he said. "I understand you know about the failure of the Marine National Bank. It has triggered quite a flurry of rumor and distrust in the city's financial community. Since I was unable to make my usual withdrawal, I felt it necessary to stay in New York and confer with my employer, to see what he wanted me to do since I could not deliver the moneys owed to our employees." He tipped his hat to the professor at this last remark. "But once that was done, I thought it wise to come and see the situation here at first hand. Better later than never, eh?"

"I suppose that's reasonable," I acknowledged.

"You may be interested to know that Monsieur Boireau is taking ship for France on Saturday. He still has extensive financial resources there, of course, but his New York holdings have been wiped out."

"I am sorry to hear it," I said, quite sincerely.

He cocked his head. "Are you?"

"Of course! I wish him no ill. I acted only on behalf of the Vanderharts. Had Monsieur Boireau not insisted on keeping his employees prisoner to preserve a needless secrecy, we would have had no quarrel at all."

"Then you had no part in sending a warship to shell his establishment on Wildwood Island?"

"None whatsoever. I am hardly the only person who took an interest in the scientists your people abducted."

"You were on the island, though."

"I was. Indeed, I did everything I could to prevent bloodshed."

"By telling our men they would not be paid and had no need to defend our property."

"Exactly. Had they not surrendered, that ship would have doubtless destroyed the entire compound."

"Or been destroyed by our own weapons."

"Mr. de la Rue, I saw that lightning generator's bolts strike the ship without doing any damage whatsoever."

De la Rue waved that aside. "You know Monsieur Boireau has fifteen other bases, even if this one is ruined."

I shrugged. "This is not my concern, unless these others are holding prisoners as this one was. I also know that some of his scientists are continuing their research despite no longer being paid, and that does not trouble me, either. If Monsieur Boireau wishes to devote his fortune to electrical research, he is certainly free to do so. It is only kidnapping and imprisonment I oppose."

"And if the people of the Lost City of the Mirage should destroy western civilization?"

"I do not think Boireau's theories are tenable, but even should he prove correct in every particular, I doubt today's events will prove crucial in any upcoming battle. Did you really think such a secret could be kept indefinitely? Do you think nothing would have been changed by the failure of the Marine National Bank?"

"One might suspect you had a hand in the bank's failure."

I snorted rudely. "Only if one is a fool. I think you'll find Messrs. Ward and Fish were responsible for it, and that I was not in any way involved, as I have never met either gentleman. Mr. de la Rue, I think you and your employer would be well advised to stop seeing conspiracies everywhere and assuming that all those who interfere with your plans are working together."

"Sometimes they *are*."

"Not all of us, I assure you. So long as you and Monsieur Boireau do not trouble me or my friends and family in the future, I have no intention of troubling *you*. I assume there will be no nonsense about retaliation or attempts to recapture the professor or myself. Remember that I have resources you have not yet discovered." I smiled. "Feel free to relay my comments to your employer. And I trust that your own salary will be made good." With that, I tipped my hat and resumed my seat.

De la Rue stared at me for a moment, then at the professor, and finally he gave Betsy a quick glance before he turned away.

The professor, Betsy, and I caught our train without incident the next morning, and after the long and wearisome ride to Camden and then New Brunswick we made our way to their home, where the entire Vanderhart family was once again reunited under their own roof. I stayed to see them all together, but remained to the side as they embraced one another. The younger children shrieked with joy to be home with their father once more; Mrs. Vanderhart wept quiet tears. Betsy embraced both her parents – her father perhaps more enthusiastically than her mother – and then moved on to her siblings.

I collected my hat from the coat rack in the front hall and raised it to the professor. "I'll be going now," I said.

"What?" Betsy turned from her younger brother Dirk and rose. "You're going?"

"I have done what I promised," I said, "and I am sure you want to spend time with your family, while I really ought to get home to my own."

"But...wait a minute, Tom." She seemed genuinely distressed.

"No, the next train is due in half an hour. I must leave now if I'm to be sure of catching it."

She hesitated, then said, "Well, let me walk with you to the station."

"If you like," I said. "I will be glad of your company." That was the simple truth; I had missed her over the past several days, and the time we had spent together since I found her waiting at the Hotel Chalfonte had hardly been enough.

"Let me get my jacket."

A moment later we walked down the front steps and turned toward the station. We came to the end of the block before either of us spoke.

"Thank you again, Tom," Betsy said at last.

I shrugged. "Your father would probably have been freed anyway, when Boireau's bank failed."

"But you were there to make sure of it. Thank you."

"I made a promise."

"Am I not to thank you for keeping it?"

"Well, you're very welcome," I said.

We walked a few more steps in silence; then she spoke again. "Tom, if you were to ask me again..."

"No," I interrupted. I knew what she was referring to. I had proposed marriage some weeks earlier in Los Angeles, and she had turned me down.

"Why not?" she asked, startled.

"Because right now you are grateful to me, deservedly or not, for your father's safe return. That may be affecting your judgment. Let us both wait until we are less influenced by recent events."

"It's not just gratitude, Tom. I missed you so much these last few days!"

"And I missed you. Nonetheless, I prefer to wait. You were right to tell me I shouldn't have asked you immediately after our escape from captivity, and I am equally certain I should not ask you now."

She did not reply immediately. We were almost to the station when she said, "I understand. And you may be right, for once."

I turned, startled, and saw her grinning up at me. I smiled back. "For once," I agreed.

At the station she stood beside me as I bought my ticket to New York, and as I turned away from the ticket window she rose up on her toes and kissed me.

Then, after a suitable time, she pulled away, smiled at me, and headed back toward he family home.

I watched her go, then hurried to catch my train.

I stayed the night at the flat on Eighteenth Street, then spent the morning of the 9th in wrapping up my business in the city, visiting Tobias Arbuthnot and Mad Bill Snedeker, and finally paying a visit to the Order of Theseus.

Sarah Darlington met me in the entry and escorted me into the main hall, where perhaps a dozen other members were in attendance; after a polite exchange of greetings I asked her, "Did you find Aubrey Elliot?"

"I did, thank you," she said.

"May I ask, where on Earth did you get that ship?"

"Oh, it belongs to Thaddeus Black," she said. "A gift from some Asiatic potentate, I believe – the Sultan of Brunei?"

"I have heard of him. I don't believe I know Mr. Black, however."

"He's a member of the Order. He does not generally operate in the Americas, though. He's made quite a fortune in more eastern lands. My understanding is that the Sultan had bought the ship, and only after the purchase was made did he discover that it was incapable of making the voyage to his homeland, so he bestowed it upon Mr. Black, who had been of service to him in some affair. I don't know the details."

"And Mr. Black loaned it to you? And provided a crew?"

"Exactly."

"That was very kind of Mr. Black to help you out so generously."

"Well, he's a friend of Alvin Hennessy and Roscoe Doolittle; Little Alvin went missing while running an errand for our friend Boireau, and Mr. Black thought he might be in that fort Boireau built." She sighed. "He wasn't, though. I hear Mr. Black intends to locate Boireau's other fifteen colonies and see whether Little Alvin is in any of them. All in all, there were eight members of the Order aboard that ship, and only five of us found whom we were looking for."

"At least five of you managed it, though."

She smiled. "That's true. Oh, by the way," she said, glancing around, "has anyone told you?"

"Told me what?" I noticed that some of the other adventurers were looking at us.

Miss Darlington raised her voice, so the rest could hear as she said, "Your application has been approved. You should be receiving an official notice, with the date of your initiation, shortly."

"Oh! Thank you."

After that there were greetings and congratulations from several others; my hand was shaken, and my back slapped, perhaps a dozen times. I was thanked more than once for bringing the newspapers to Wildwood Island, and preventing bloodshed or further destruction, though there were others who seemed to regret losing the opportunity to see just what Black's monitor and Boireau's electrical devices could do.

I was also questioned about what I knew of Monsieur Boireau's theories, and whether I thought he was correct in believing the Lost City of the Mirage was a serious threat to us all. I repeated every time that I had no idea whether his theories had any factual basis, but I did point out what I saw as the more obvious problems in them.

And finally, around mid–afternoon, I escaped to Grand Central Terminal, where I boarded a train for home. I had not seen my mother or sister in many months, and I thought it was well past time to remedy that.

– THE END –

The New-York Times.

VOL. XXXIII.....NO. 10,194.   NEW-YORK, WEDNESDAY, MAY 7, 1884.

WALL STREET STARTLED

THE MARINE NATIONAL BANK CLOSES ITS DOORS.

CAUSING THE SUSPENSION OF THE FIRM OF GRANT & WARD, OF WHICH PRESIDENT FISH WAS A PARTNER.

Startling rumors swept through Wall-street at noon yesterday, and for an hour messengers from banking houses and broker's offices were kept flying hither and thither in quest of accurate information. That the Marine National Bank had closed its doors was soon ascertained. The news that followed was even more sensational. Grant & Ward, bankers and brokers, No. 2 Wall-street, announced their suspension, and ugly stories of an unaccountable deficiency of half a million dollars arose.

The fact that ex-President Grant was interested, with his son, in the embarrassed firm became speedily known, and expressions of sympathy were heard on every hand. Ferdinand Ward, one of the active partners, it was said, had dragged the firm down by his extensive real estate speculations with James D. Fish, President of the broken bank. "The Street" needed but to learn that Mr. Ward was a Director of the bank and Mr. Fish a special partner in the firm of Grant & Ward to jump at the conclusion that the double disaster was from a single cause.

The feeling in and about the Stock Exchange was very feverish for a short time, and until it was definitely learned that the affairs of the bank

Bank was indebted
that the reason of
unknown to the D
could imagine was
The bank, it was
as its last statemen
claimed to be wort
tion upon the boo
unanimous in stati
ties had been ma
carrying any doubt
ble exception of (
it was explained, l
full significance
existing between
Grant & Ward, i
a large business
at a low rate of i
time at a higher r
stood that the fi
$2,000,000, and tha
were to pay off
called in. "I sup
able to realize up
them as collateral
Elwell, "and the
tated. The stor
volved the bar
or that he is hopel
lieve. Mr. Fish in
he had made $600,(
estate operations,
speculated in sto
time past."

The Directors c
among the heavie
present having $
fully $500,000 belo
board now locked

The relations be
Ward and the Mar
ly after the forma
of 1880. The conce
Gen. U. S. Grant,
Ward, James D. F
Grant became a
The capital was
of which was

About the Author:

Lawrence Watt-Evans has been a full-time writer for more than forty years, with more than fifty novels and well over a hundred short stories to his credit, as well as assorted essays, poems, comic books, and so on. His story "Why I Left Harry's All-Night Hamburgers" won the 1988 Hugo for short story, as well as the Asimov's Readers Award. He lives in Bainbridge Island, Washington with his wife.

His website is at www.watt-evans.com.

www.ingramcontent.com/pod-product-compliance
Lightning Source LLC
Chambersburg PA
CBHW070745180626
46818CB00007B/2998